in memory of my brother, Louis

chapter 1

[1]

NOW I'VE STEPPED ON a *rusty fucking nail*. Not my first, either. Three nails at three different locations have pierced the soles of three unrelated shoes. And this happens to everybody who wanders out. I have to keep a First-Aid kit in my van for this type of thing. "Kit" is inadequate, and too short a word.

There's a little window period with Tetanus, of about twenty-four hours. Or so I was told by Mrs. G., a woman with a camper truck, who drove the neighborhoods, passing out vaccines.

[2]

I have this friend, Lucien, not a friend so much as he's my intern, who's been going around with me for months, every weekday, for a good part of the day.

Although, there is little left to our job.

Ah, but you carry on here as if nothing could ever really be over.

[3]

There was work once before the work went out of town. You could do a lot of location scouting here. Everyone wanted you to. They hurled money at you, the production people with so much money, who wanted to film here because of the tax incentives, or the nine months of shooting weather, or the easy attitude toward permits, or because the place can mimic any other place that a film crew, then, *wouldn't have to go.*

I still get work, oh sure, and the New Orleans film industry isn't 100 percent in the shitter. I get commercials, or they're not quite commercials. These one- or two-day shoots. They're more like change-of-address ads. The businesses want to announce they still exist. They've relocated maybe, but they're back up, open.

[4]

So Lucien, my intern all this time, day-after-day for months, turns and says to me, "My name's *Paul.*"

[5]

I'm not from here and I'll probably never get used to things, but I doubt if I'll ever leave. A rest might be an idea. There's too much eating. There's altogether too much sex, dancing, carousing, reveling. All of it goes on for far too long. There's powdered sugar dust on everything. There are twinkle lights burning every day of the year. Funerals, Jell-O shots, fishing, swearing, barbecues, back-door gigs, vats and vats of jambalaya. There are too many houses and sidewalks disappearing under weeds and vines and in yards that look impenetrable, too many neon signs, too much on-the-stoop drinking, corruption, and Technicolor clothes, too much Crawfish shucking, and Catholic everything, too much stale beer, too many heroin junkies shooting up on the balconies, too many big homes, and trees snapped off, too many steel billboards bent to the ground, too much andouille sausage, too many second lines, too much money, and debauch, and cars parked all crooked.

"Do you never *tire?*" I cry from the car window.

[6]

My husband is from here. So is his twin. They're a couple of rummies with money to burn. I've been married eight years to my husband. He wasn't my first; I wasn't his, what of it?

[7]

Ease and Comfort

- Holstered guns are worn under your clothing, close to the skin. The holster's waterproof padding will protect your gun from body moisture and perspiration.

- The side of a holster that faces out is broader so your gun won't imprint an outline through your clothes.

- A rigid-walled holster will allow you to put your gun away easily, with one hand. Flexible models can collapse after you draw, requiring both hands and more time to reholster.

[8]

Here they are now, the twins Rags & Gasoline, lounging on their parents' veranda in the shade of a blue jacaranda tree.

They are dressed exactly alike again today, and that is one of the many ways they entertain themselves. I've been standing at a little distance, watching, and I wouldn't bet a dime on my guessing which is which.

Now a man in white linen appears on the veranda with a tray. It has coffee in mugs, honey and biscuits, a bottle of English whiskey.

"Whose turn is to be my husband?" I ask, stepping up. To the man serving the breakfast tray, I say, "Not you. Or, not necessarily. Only if you want."

[9]

I found out a little while ago that my husband has Hep-C. It's symptomless! And yet, he has an active strain. He could be lying! He isn't, though.

"It's all right," he says now, with a hand patting my back. "I feel good. Be just fine. It's really everything all right."

I say, "Well, goddamn you."

"Underway," says he.

[10]

It's not great, the deal Adam has with his parents. It takes care of some bits of business, in that they pay for everything. They provide nurses, and a dietician. They paid to get him onto a transplant list. But he has to live here, with them, all the time.

I think sometimes: "He's only forty-two and he's this sick!"

Or, I think: "He's forty-two and he's had to run home to his parents!"

While I'm left kind of standing at the corner. And where, above me, it would seem, there's a very red light.

[11]

Saunders is the other twin, utterly identical. That's a good thing about him. Also to his credit are his wife and his little girl.

The bad things include an array of incidents, arrests, brawls, screaming, wretched Western Union transactions, also, all the clubs, bars, saloons, hotels, private homes, city parks, businesses, establishments, and streets he's been asked to leave.

[12]

Thirty Months After Katrina

- NOPD's crime lab was destroyed and has not been replaced.

- There is 1 fingerprint examiner.

- More than 2000 evidence tests are backlogged.

- The department still has no headquarters, and officers operate out of FEMA trailers, even the brass.

- The trailers are not air-conditioned. In hot months, officers do reports and paperwork in their cars.

- There's no place for storing evidence. It too is kept in trailers, unprotected.

- There's no place for interviewing witnesses and victims, no place for interrogating suspects.

- NOPD's guns were destroyed during the storm. Police officers often have to provide their own guns and ammo.

[13]

I just can't manage the switch. It's undoable. Two days of correcting myself after every Lucien thought with "You mean Paul. Paul. It's Paul. Who's actually Lucien. Think of him as Paul."

[14]

"You look different," he says now.

I try this: "No. I don't."

He asks, "Aren't you ordinarily wearing a hat?"

"No, I'm never wearing a hat. Not one single time. I don't even own any."

"Well, something's weird then, because I *remember* you in different hats. Especially the two I liked best," says he.

I say, "I'm about to smash you in the shoulder blades."

"Vividly, I remember," he says. "There were two that I favored over all your other headgear."

"Lucien," I say, without reluctance or regret.

[15]

Drowsily, the husband lifts up in bed. He reaches and searches the end table for the TV remote.

"It's right here," I say, showing him I have it.

There are noises through the open windows from a cypress forest behind the house. Spiky shadows knife the walls in here, and there's a sweet odor from some fruit tree or other. We have only a snapping, inconsistent light from the television screen and its *Mr. Moto* movie.

He eases out of the sheets, and sits on the side of the bed. In the dim, his bare chest shines and his boxer shorts blink the whitest white.

Neither of us used to sleep through 'til morning. We would take naps together, at this time of the evening. We would wake up and play around, put on music, drink, go back to sleep, awaken.

We'd have whiskey in tea, and sweet potato muffins.

"Hit channel thirty," he tells me now.

Outside the room are powdery-white hallways, arched doors, a carved staircase. It would seem an enormous, lovely house where you could sit in an alcove on a bench and read, but it isn't.

I turn down the TV volume and switch around in my seat. "O.K., this is thirty. What are we tuning in?"

"Like you're staying," he says.

There is work waiting for me, true. Work that'll keep me busy tonight, some of tomorrow. *Work*, though, that I would rather not go and do.

Longing and resentment. Some of both in the way my husband is stamping out his cigarette.

[16]

I've motored out the Great River Road toward Bayou Lafourche below Napoleonville. Here, I will see what I can see.

You have to get up on the levee for a view of anything. Down by the river, there's a pearly dawn over the blazing water, and an egret acting drunk on the banks. Otherwise, not a lot going on.

Here are a couple guys, however, waltzing along.

"Do you know anything about the riverboat schedules?" I ask.

"No," from these two, who are trying to act nonchalant, and as if they don't live their lives in various abandoned vehicles.

[17]

Some Things, You Finish With and They're Over

- Yesterday, for the last time in my life, I cleaned a broiler pan.

- I'm never again wearing anything bought at Lowe's.

- I'm done drinking boilermakers.

- Spinning until dizzy on barstools is a thing of the past.

- No more pawning my luggage.

[18]

"Completion bonds," I'm telling Lucien. We're somewhere, parked in my location-scouting van. I'm giving a lesson.

He says, "Does this have partly to do with a deaf couple and Tom Cruise?"

"Nothing to do with them."

"Go on then," says Lucien.

"Completion bonds are something a film company acquires in advance. Then, if a production doesn't finish filming on time, the money people don't get fucked by the over-budget expenses. I guess the bonding people get fucked instead, but they must expect that to happen from time to time. It's just insurance, O.K.? You see what I mean?"

Lucien nods a few times while drawing on a cigarette. Now he holds it as though his hand is very, very tired.

"After Katrina," I say, "no one was willing to write completion bonds. Your thing's about to drip ashes there, amigo. Nobody would, and that's one of the biggest reasons the film companies took a hike."

"Ma'am?" says Lucien, and I'll want to speak to him about that later on.

"Just let me get through this," I say.

He settles back on the passenger seat, his smoking hand now dangled out the window. He watches me dully, as if he'll soon be going to sleep.

I say, "Even a more serious problem, is what went *with* the production companies on their way out of town. The crew base. We have a diminished and devalued crew base. Where you need a depth of three or four individuals in each and every skill. We're down to one individual for some skills, and, for most skills, no individuals."

"That's sad," Lucien says.

"Yep," I say, turning the engine.

He says, "You know what I think we should do? Like, immediately? Or, never mind. I'm not even going to suggest anything."

"You're welcome to."

"No. Maybe you just better ignore me," he says, as if that would not have occurred to me to do.

[19]

Hell, it's a lucky day if I'm photographing real estate. Things will never get back. I'm out of business, and I ought to fucking move.

What I do now, day in and day out, is all hypothetical. I've become a "what-if" location scout.

[20]

In a City That Is Only Seven Miles Long

• Alcoholic beverages are available 24 hours a day, 7 days a week.

• Alcohol is the leading cause of death for Louisiana youth.

• Drinking in the street is acceptable and legal, although not from a glass or a bottle.

• Bars and clubs provide plastic go-cup containers.

• Most have walk-up windows for refills.

• More undergraduates die from alcohol-related causes
   than the number who receive advanced degrees.

[21]

The twins' mother will say to me, at various times, she'll say, "Don't
count on it," or "Don't be too sure." She can respond this way on
any subject. Whatever happens, whatever information I receive from
anyone, the mother-in-law is there beside me, saying, "If you can put
any faith in that," or, "You'd like to think so," or, "So I'm sure they
would have you believe."

   "Don't you wish," she has said to me, and "Don't tell me you
fell for that one." She'll ask me, "Are you thinking clearly? *When* are
you going to stop kidding yourself?" and say, "It amazes me you're
so easily persuaded. You bought that one outright. Dream on. Dream
away. You couldn't be in your right mind. Have you lost all sense of
proportion?"

[22]

"The way it works is," I'm telling Lucien, "they send us a script or
script treatment. We peruse it and come up with whatever location
ideas we can. Then our fees are based on their budget and on what
type of production they're doing. They either pay us a day rate, or
they can get a package deal that includes Prep days, Shooting days,

and Strike days when we clean up the property. You have that? There are three classifications. A small still shoot with ten crew. A medium commercial with forty. Or a feature film with over a hundred."

He says, "Check. Got it. Small, medium, big. Now, I keep meaning to ask you and then I always forget. How do they decide about the amount we're getting paid?"

"Well," I say, "it's interesting. First, they are set rates. The rates for the package deal and the day rate. Set. I mean, in cement. And the day rate, at first blush, is going to seem high, because it's three grand a day, or however much. But some companies will go ahead and agree to that, knowing they're going to work you nineteen- or twenty-hour days, one day after another. When there's nothing, at that point, you can do."

"Three grand as in three thousand?"

"But where you still end up feeling—"

"Like they're fully exploited," Lucien says. "Taking every advantage of."

"Well, you're not wrong," I say.

[23]

The twins' family business is one of prevailing and owning. They keep offices where they never go to do nothing. That is how they hold onto all the leftover wealth that was left to them, by utilizing skills I wasn't ever meant to understand.

[24]

"Your parents have money," I say and pause.

Adam's waiting for me to continue. "They do," he says. "With you so far."

I say, "I'm getting there, give me a second. This has to be said in order."

"Albeit, at a crawl," says Saunders.

"Can't we do this out of his earshot?" I ask.

"Just," Adam says, "go."

"Everybody in contact with your parents, tries to endear her or himself."

"Way to pronoun," Saunders says.

I say, "If I may. My point being—"

"That's all right," says Adam. "I got your point. You cleared a lot of things up for me."

"It's just that if I were sweet and pleasant around your parents, they'd file that behavior in a category, and then they'd assign it a motive."

"Yes, she's quite right. They'd *know* it was a trick and that something was horribly wrong," Saunders says.

[25]

I tried not working and staying "home" at Adam's parents' house for the first few weeks of our marriage.

I would spend mornings and afternoons in their library, and keep reading as long as I could, then dine with them usually, but then get out of the way, put on a nightshirt, take a stack of books up to bed with me at 7 or 8 P.M.

They could keep to themselves, that way. They could keep their privacy, keep one another's counsel, keep private their long whispery talks about being rich, being them, being other things that I'm not.

[26]

I confided in my new sister-in-law back then, Saunders' wife, Petal. I said at the beginning of the month I'd go back to work and move Adam into an apartment. "So we can have our own place, because I do want to stay married to him," I said.

"It's your life, your vagina," said Petal.

"You mean I'm somehow wasting myself on him? How could you think that? You're married to his twin."

"Umm, it's just different," she said.

"Let me guess. You two are younger."

"Cold," she said. "I'm older, and Saunders and Adam were born the same night."

"Of course, of course. Then the difference is that Saunders—I mean, I like him."

She said, "We all do."

"Although, he really does drink—Adam less so—all day. Every, every day."

"Nothing I can call untrue," Petal said.

"But that's still not it, is it," I said. "Then, I don't know what. Are the two of them very different in bed?"

"I've never had reason to ask them," Petal said.

I said, "Picture me with the bar of soap later, washing out my mouth."

"Things are just different," she said, "when you have a child."

[27]

Those days, my job was very pleasant, a pleasant kind of going around, snapping pictures of various landscapes, wandering through buildings, and over parks, observatories, school grounds, scouting the neighborhoods, learning all the dope, sitting in on things. The agency shouldn't have paid me. I could have done all that for free. They should have asked how my day went. Perhaps, very carefully recorded my answer. Then they should have said, "Super. Great. Thanks a big bunch. Stop by again tomorrow and we can have another chat."

[28]

The Way You Look Tonight

• Thigh Holsters are good when you want to Open Carry.
  A holster on the thigh puts your gun under your hand.
  Most have pop buckles for instant access.

- In Louisiana, you do not need a permit to Open Carry.

- In Louisiana, you may Open Carry at any time in your vehicle.

- You must be 21 to purchase a gun in Louisiana. However, a gun that was a gift is legal.

- In Louisiana, the minimum age for Open Carrying is 17.

chapter 2

To Lucien, I say: "You're always asking me these difficult questions. They're difficult and they are several. And while I'm standing here, let me ask *you*. Are there more things you haven't divulged to me? Like that you've had the wrong name."

"Ah, don't believe so. No," he says.

"Well, I knew that you'd say that. But concentrate now. What else haven't you told me?"

"I'm trying to think," he says.

"And?"

He says, "I do keep the dogs. Seven dogs. If that doesn't have to be a secret."

"They're your dogs?"

"Yes'm, they're mine."

"Live dogs that live with you. Seven in number."

He says, "There are seven. Unless my grandma narrowed it down to six."

"Who's your grandma? I mean, where are your folks?"

"Uh, deceased," says Lucien. "But it's not 'cause she's my grandma that I live with her."

"Right, whatever that means," I say.

He says, "My clothes. That's something you don't know about. I spend all my money on clothes."

I'm smiling, and instantly not smiling, regretting the two seconds I was. I thought Lucien's wardrobe involved clothes he just had.

I thought maybe he'd spent the night at a friend's, borrowed pants and shirts, wore them thereafter. Or that he'd gone on a road trip, stopped by a trucker's place, grabbed the last items on the rack. I thought perhaps he took control of a neighbor's clothes after the neighbor evacuated. Or that he might have inherited clothing from a cousin who lost a lot of weight.

[30]

"I don't like how paranoid you're getting," I say to my husband.

"Well, in order to think that, you'd have to be scrutinizing my every move."

"This here is what I mean," I say.

[31]

Crawling on all fours over there by the coffee table is Saunders, the Sack twin of my husband, Save. Saunders is perhaps merely looking for a contact lens. I'm certainly not going to ask him. He'd engage me in an answer. Besides which, he probably doesn't know.

[32]

'Round Midnight

- Over 70 percent of New Orleans musicians remain displaced.
- Many of them are living in their cars.
- Friends who gutted the flooded homes of fellow musicians reported a terrible loss of instruments, including hundreds of ruined grand pianos.

[33]

I'm not going to be able to manage with these people and the things they do.

Collie, for example, my niece, was this morning a little girl, wearing a smock and her carrot hair in two long braids, come to visit her grandmother. Then the grandmother whisked her off and took her someplace where clothes are turned pink and braids chopped and heads shorn and left looking like sprouting pineapples.

I could smack that grandmother unconscious and roll her out into the yard. She could stay out there a good while, pondering the harm she's done.

Petal has arrived to pick up the kid.

She stares straight ahead after experiencing a view of the haircut.

I say, "Let us sit down here and smoke bags of dope at the dining table."

The room twinkles around us with snowy linen and crystal-dripping chandeliers.

"One thing you could do is kill your husband," I say. "He deserves it for being her son."

"I was already going to, for other reasons," Petal says.

"Adam?" she asks, halfway changing the subject.

"Exists," I say with a nod.

"So, where are they?" she asks. "They should be down here, shouldn't they?"

I shake my head. "I can't speak for all wives about all husbands. Only for me, about mine. He is far too fucked to participate in this situation."

The dope is burning a hole in my pocket. I keep offering it but nobody takes me up.

The room, the chandelier light, the sad face on Petal, the sounds of the night coming on, the smells from the gardens around this palace, my longing, her longing.

⌈34⌋

The mother appears with a handsome silver teapot and pours from it without speaking to us at all. Her mouth is fresh with crimson lipstick. Her hair's tucked behind a calfskin band. Her eyes shift left and right below her lowered lashes.

She introduces a platter with ice chunks, lettuce leaves, a thousand Gulf shrimp.

I close my eyes and rest my head on the back of my chair. She's here now and there's no more use in thinking. She's brought enough tension and misery to last the three of us for hours.

⌈35⌋

"Good Night Nurse in the fourth," Saunders says. "Lady's Man in the fifth. Definitely. In the sixth, Wild Lightning. Then, some of these others, I still haven't decided. Cosmo! Any fucking race he runs."

"What about Soldier Boy?" Petal asks. "I thought you were so impressed with him."

"Nah." Saunders shakes his head. "Not anymore. I went down there and took a look at him last time. 'Cause, you know, I had won big money."

"We *both* went," Adam says, angling his chair so he can face Saunders. "To see Soldier Boy. You don't remember?"

"Yeah, O.K., it was both of us." Saunders nods. To Petal, and me he says, "Utterly psychotic."

"I mean the horse," he adds, because we're both eyeing him.

Adam says, "Oh, that was all drug induced, that we witnessed. Clearly a drugged up animal."

"I don't care," Saunders says. "He was foaming. He was slobbering."

"Drooling drool," says Adam.

"Playing with his own manure," Saunders says.

"All right, don't be little babies," Petal tells them.

To me, she says, "Foaming, slobbering, playing with their own manure."

[36]

• I'm through reading lengthy bits of scripture into the answering machines of my enemies.

• I'm saying goodbye to Sloppy Joes.

• No more Foosball.

• I'm done hiding up in a tree.

• No more soaking cigarettes in little bowls of paregoric.

[37]

We've stopped in at a Waffle House, Lucien and I. It's our first occasion being together outside the van. He looks different, naturally, seated opposite. I'm gazing at him, getting his face instead of his profile. Looking too hard, perhaps. Causing him to check his reflection in the glass between these booths and the team of grill cooks.

I think it might help to mention the husband. "I have a husband," I say.

"I know, I *met* the two of them," Lucien says.

"Well, there's only one, for the moment, but it can certainly seem otherwise."

"So, is this man your first marriage?"

"No," I say, "it isn't. But I still try to keep it, you know, one at a time."

He says, "Now, didn't I hear that your husband's sick with a health problem?"

I'm really not sure if yes is the answer, but I give it as one either way.

"And, someone might've also told me, that he's been that way a long time?"

"Years and years, it turns out," I say.

There's a guy leaning on the bathroom door over there, asking, "Melissa? Melissa. Are you *sure* you're O.K.?"

[38]

The twins' parents are from Cornsilk, Louisiana and they met in Cornsilk, Louisiana. For some special wedding anniversary they bought a boxer dog named Snaps.

[39]

We're in a front parlor at the twins' parents' place. Petal's on a red leather couch before the tall doors to the terrace. One of the doors hangs open and she's motioning her cigarette smoke outside. Without conviction. With no real success.

The room has embroidered pillows, flowers in Italian urns.

The wind changes and rain sprays in. Petal reaches behind her and bats the door closed.

I'm wet. I've been outside where it's raining. My hair's streaming. My stockings are glistened. My shoes are sopped and weigh like turkeys.

It will stop in a minute. The sky does this—opens and drops another load on the city—every motherfucking day.

Petal's in crisp white and navy, lounging on the couch arm, with her legs up under her. She dusts the arm for cigarette ash, clears her throat. She says, "You know, one of the twin spans has been rated critical. I think it's the westbound, got a two. On a one-through-nine rating scale."

I say, "I noticed the pitiful patch job they did."

Saunders rolls in and takes a seat on the couch with Petal. He says, "They knew full well the bearings were beat to shit." He notices my wetness, gives me a smirk.

"I'll get to it," I say.

Petal and I are often different when Drag & Drop are around. We speak less often, and say less when we do. I don't understand why. They're only a couple of men.

He says, "I read they tried using bridge jacks to support the ones that're the worst. Only *then*, I read another thing, said the bearings aren't even the problem. Although, they're utter garbage, no question. But, supposedly, the girders and pilings are what's really terrifying."

"The eastbound's not much better," says Petal. "It got, I think, a three."

"Yeah. That's so," Saunders says, nodding. And staring outside, he says, "There it goes again. The goddamn dog, diving into the pond."

"What'll it do? Eat the swans?" I ask.

"I don't think it's focused enough to catch a swan," says Saunders. "It'll just stand there in the water, barking at them. Which Father will pretend, all afternoon, he doesn't hear. When it's entirely his responsibility, 'cause it's his fuckhead dog. But Adam always ends up being the one taking care of it."

"He's too sick to go into the pond, though," I say with a shake of the head.

"Yeah," Saunders says. "He's too sick."

[40]

On the grounds of the parents' place are winding paths that lead under magnolia trees and under Live Oaks, with branches that reach and meet overhead.

One path follows a drive to the front gate. Another path leads to the pond.

The twins' sister, Julia, drowned herself in that water. No one's ever said why, and I wasn't around, and didn't know her, so

I wouldn't know. But I don't like that place. It's got a statue the parents had made—a white stone statue of a girl set about shin-deep in the pool. Then the father added two black swans. They swim in an endless circle.

People will pause along the wrought-iron fence for a glimpse of the statue. The neighbor kids are always there, always fooling around. They throw stuff, pelt it with stones and sticks, command it to move.

[41]

Guardians of Our Health

- Only 1 of the 7 general hospitals is fully operational. 2 are partially open. 4 remain closed.

- The number of hospital beds remains down by 80 percent. Hospitals refuse people.

- Anybody they can't refuse is given sedatives and left on a gurney in the hall.

- There are no orthopedists. For broken bones, the recommended treatment spot is Houston.

- New Orleans has been unable to fluoridate its tap water since the storm.

[42]

Here I am, in the place where my husband left me. If things stay like this, I don't know what I'll do.

The day's thundershower is over. My power's not out. There's nothing whatsoever to keep me from vacuuming.

[43]

Saunders needs monitoring today. Petal's in Jamaica or somewhere and she asked me to go over, check on her husband, make sure everything's O.K.

So, here's his car, parked catawampus at the foot of the driveway. From this point, I can trace his every trip, stumble, and fall.

He gets out, goes a little way up the drive, veers off, collides with these shrubs and crushes them to hell. Here's his key chain, and his keys, anybody wants them. Drops his white handkerchief also. I'm sure his wallet's on the ground here too. Then he trips over the newspaper basket, topples onto a bench, knocks that on its back. Comes to again, gets up, finally makes it to the door, but no keys, he can't get in. Bashes the doorknob with a rock several times. That does nothing. Breaks the window with the rock, throws it somewhere. Reaches in, works the knob, bloodies his hand but gets the door open, and ah, here he is, utterly unconscious, one, two, three feet inside.

[44]

Now Saunders is awake and at his parents' place, where I chauffeured him. He's ending an argument with me by saying, "You snaking snake. Snaking up my trouser leg."

"She wouldn't go *near* your trouser leg," says Adam.

"Well, that's unless," I say, "I don't know. If there were anything that might—"

"Wouldn't," says Adam, wagging his head at me, "go near."

[45]

Niece Collie wants me to dress up with her and go out in the neighborhood. Sing songs with her, all the many, many songs she knows. She asks my favorite everything. Favorite animal, favorite month, car, vegetable, holiday, favorite smell, favorite saying, taste, flower, sound, favorite star, favorite coin, my favorite piece of chicken.

"I have to quit talking with you now," I finally tell her. "Because it's the nighttime, when everyone else, everywhere, is already asleep."

Seersucker pajamas, yellow with a cactus print.

She's tugged off the pillowcase. Pulls it on over her head and leans close to my face.

I say, "You can stay that way. Just like that for the whole night. Doesn't intimidate me."

[46]

I'm idling in the driveway after dropping off Collie.

"If there's anything missing," Petal says, crouching outside the car window.

"In my marriage?"

"No," she says, "I mean, if you're looking around and you think something's gone."

I shake my head. "That . . . doesn't make sense to me."

"All right," she says. "Suppose there's a time, after Collie's stayed over, when you're trying hard to find something, and you can't."

"Now I get it," I say, clunking off my car's engine, the better to hear.

"You don't need to get upset," Petal says. "Nothing is, in fact, gone. She just has it hidden. Sometimes, she'll even wrap things up in paper like presents and then she'll give them right back to you."

"Collie steals stuff?"

"S'what I'm saying," says Petal

[47]

"I never know what to call you," Lucien says.

My chin is nodding, my mouth tacked. "It's a little bit of a problem."

He says, "You sign everything 'E.' but, honestly, *I* would feel like a half-wit if I called you E."

"Can understand that," I say. "Ev is fine. My husband calls me Ev." I exhale. "It's Eve, all right? My name's Eve, married to Adam."

"Oh."

"Now you know," I say. "Our names really didn't bother me that much until the mail started arriving addressed to 'Adam and Eve Broussard'."

"I *hail* from Broussard," says Lucien, and lowering his voice, and raising an index finger, he says, "I do! Like the very back end of Broussard. I mean the backest-back."

"Or the endest-end," I say.

"That's me," he says.

He asks, "So, why did you even marry Adam? You should have steered clear of a man with that name. Or did he just bowl you over without realizing it?"

I say, "Well, that sounds like the right explanation. Although, not terribly fair to me."

"What I'll never understand," he says, "is how you decided to pick which one. They're identically alike! With no difference between them! At least, not so far as the naked eye."

[48]

- I'm through putting Xeroxes of dollar bills into change machines.

- No more drinking from the milk cartons in the dairy section of the store.

- I'm never again burping the alphabet.

- No more wearing white stockings and being anybody's nurse.

- No more stories about ever having been a Carmelite nun.

[49]

Adam takes a seat beside me now on a pique-covered settee. He sits straight, his knees apart, and across his lap rests his walking cane, thing, ridiculous stick.

"That is for an old man," I say to him.

In a quiet voice he tells me, "Well, I have the liver of a very old man."

"Ah."

"It's simply true," he says. "We need to house what's true in our heads. Don't you think that?"

"Hell no," I say. "There's so much bad news and imagery I don't want in my mind. Hell fucking no. Including this picture I now have of you with a throbbing and decayed old liver. Just what good is that supposed to do me?"

He's holding the cane almost timidly now.

Looking at me with a little chagrin. What eyes those are, that he has.

[50]

Here's an unexplained man with a bandaged shoulder, asleep right on the sidewalk at the intersection.

What else could be done to this place, I wonder, besides tipping it over and pouring it out?

I guess the pipes in the earth below us—weakened and wrenched and corroded as they are from the hammering of the storm and the weeks of stewing in saltwater—could split and tear and crack open and leak raw sewage into the water supply.

[51]

Here we've got eighteen people, seated in Lafayette Square, whomping empty soda cans on the pavement, all of them chanting all the while, "Let's be Jesus. Let's be Jesus 'til it hurts. Let's be Yawa—"

[52]

You could fill your time easily, going around and noticing this type of shit. Such as there, dragging along, is a woman wearing one bare foot and the other in a satin dinner slipper.

[53]

• My address book is nowhere to be found,

• nor my jean jacket,

• the box of coffee filters,

• the good cookbook,

• the tiny ballerina from my childhood jewelry box,

• my gymbag,

• a rhinestone-studded belt,

• the globe!

chapter 3

[54]

LUCIEN'S INVITED OVER later to go through ideas for more local commercials. I've scribbled a few driving directions for him, to get to my
place on Julia Street.

He says, "This'll help. The Warehouse District, right? This is
where you live?"

"Yeah, it is. Sort of," I say.

He glances over.

"The address is fine, and correct," I tell him. "I'm not at all confused about where."

[55]

"It does seem peculiar," says Lucien, "that you have your TV turned
fully on, but with no *sound*."

I say, "There's a special ability I developed, by way of staying awake too long. Even with the sound muted, I can hear Mariska Hargitay."

"I'm O.K. with that," he says. "But, however. Who you got on here now is Anderson Cooper."

"God bless his sweet heart," I say.

I say, "And he and Mariska Hargitay aren't incompatible."

"I'm just worried," Lucien says. "I'm afraid you could miss a critical thing he's reporting."

"That's a good worry. The fact that you have it is a reason you work for me and not for Republicans."

Lucien nods and accepts this and rolls away and goes back to what he was doing—making faces at himself in a little compact mirror. I have no idea why.

[56]

Here are the twins, I've Seen Fire & I've Seen Rain, propped on their sides on the bed, a chessboard between them; both shirtless, both gazing hard at the board.

I think my husband's the one in pajama bottoms, and the other is just wearing jeans.

"It's the Vietnamese who own the place now," Saunders is saying. "And, do you know, everything they've done, they did it with private money."

"Turns out there's no other kind," Adam says, or the one I think is Adam.

To me, he says, "How's it doin', Boonsfarm?"

[57]

In their joint ownership—they have chosen now to show me—is a shoebox filled with cocaine.

"We just need you to be aware of it," Adam says.

"In case something should happen," says Saunders.

He says, "Do not, I repeat, do not tell Petal."

"Like what're you afraid will happen?" I ask.

"Let's close our eyes and let our minds wander," he says.

"O.K.," I say. "Of course, right, of course. Cat Four hurricane. No wetlands to absorb it. Floods crashing. Tinker-toy levees crumbling to bits. Water rising in a hurry. No one is coming. Shots fired. Slow cooking on a roof, and dying of thirst for days—"

"Sing it, sister," Adam says.

I say, "None of that's going to occur."

"Wow," Saunders says, his arms crossed and his eyebrows lifted.

"But suppose we were to experience that scenario," I say. "The plan is then, for me to stay behind here and guard all your cocaine?"

[58]

Adam wandered out a bit ago and I've taken his place on the bed across from Saunders. I pluck up one of Adam's chess pieces, the queen's bishop, is my best guess, and move it idly forward. Saunders studies the board a second, snatches the bishop and stamps it back on its square."

"I've never really had cocaine," I say.

"Wait, stop, back up," I tell Saunders as he starts a grin. "That wasn't said right. It should have been, never done cocaine. Or, never *used* it."

"Welcome to the city, Miss Near-Beer," he says.

"So, it was Houston cocaine?" I ask, and add, "That's what the newspapers intimated," before he can mock me any further way.

"In fact," says Saunders, his eyes still on the board. "Truckloaded to us daily. Available at any of the open-air drug markets, uptown or down. Fortunately, you're offered a kind of trial subscription, if you aren't completely sure at first how much you want to invest."

He lifts a pawn off the board, lowers it back down.

"Aren't you worried about the illegality?" I ask him.

He shakes his head no. "It's no longer any different from *legality*," he says. He raises a hand and counts off on his fingers: "Witnesses don't come forward. The police don't gather evidence. The prosecutor doesn't indict. Juries never convict anybody."

I blink at him.

"What? It's not my fucking fault," he says. "Except, it is my fault, same as it's everybody's. But then, down below us, way down where no clean air gets in, there are those whose faults it truly is."

I say, "You're making it sound as though everyone's a fuckup."

He shrugs, moves out a knight. "What can I tell you?"

"All that is parenthetical," I say. "Witnesses only clam up because they know the perps will get right back out. Police probably do gather evidence. There's no one to examine it, at least, not in time. Prosecutors can't indict and juries can't convict without evidence."

Saunders' head bobs in thought. He reaches and knocks over his queen. "You forgot to mention," he says, "that Katrina drained the jury pool. Plus the fact there aren't any public defenders. So how are you gonna go to trial?"

Adam comes back in and leans on a bedpost.

I say, "Meanwhile, y'awl are snorting cocaine. Isn't that a great piece of news."

I say, "I sense that 'snorting' is the wrong verb, possibly. So, what, then? You don't have holes in your arms. Don't answer! Motherfuckers! This is what I most hate. You're making me drool on myself."

"Now you're furious," says Adam.

Saunders says, "We haven't—"

"No, don't tell me, " I say. "Fuck that. Fuck telling me anything. We'll all just keep quiet."

[59]

I had a different husband in the late '90s. Charlie. He was a professor of neuroscience, from a harbor town in northeast Ireland. We were fine being married. For over two years, we were fine. Then one day his mother was thrown from a train that collided with another train on its way to Connolly Station. So, Charlie went home to take care of his mom, and we would talk on the phone every few days. I thought he'd say something, eventually, about returning to the states. He never did, though. His mother was pretty much broken to bits. A widow. And Charlie had a much younger sister. We stopped calling back and forth so often, he and I. Until it became once or twice a month, once a month, every two or three months that we'd talk. Then I dragged myself through divorcing him. It was sad.

[60]

I should have offered to join Charlie in Ireland, and offered to help him take care of his mom. Helped with his sister. He must have waited for me to do that. While all I could think was, When's he going to wrap it up and come home?

There that is. Written right on me. Never, ever to be scratched out.

[61]

Up the Lazy River

- New Orleans has the highest incarceration rate of any major U.S. city.

- Cases typically take three years to go to trial.

- 88 percent of those who are charged qualify as indigent.

- 1 in 7 African Americans is imprisoned.

- Penal institutions are paid per inmate in Louisiana, and financially rewarded for high occupancy.

- The state legislature has now barred lawsuits by individuals kept in prison beyond their release dates.

[62]

The father is speaking to Petal and me, and has been for thirty or forty minutes, going on and on about living with disappointments, and how he's learned to live with so many, and other sourceless claims he's making, that he ought to be embarrassed about, and that we really shouldn't listen to, if we're doing the right thing.

"Ladies, are you getting my message?" he asks when neither of us will look at him or respond in any way.

"Check," says Petal.

Now as a pile of fudge desert is served her, she says, "So, I could have some of this instead of teeth."

[63]

Lucien's standing there at an angle like a stylish woman, his weight on one leg, a hand on his hip. He's gazing through a pair of horn rims at our task sheet.

Making up the task sheet is somebody's job, so I want to respect that and help the person stay on the payroll, even though she or he has nothing to do. The sheet has wordy descriptions of tasks we're to perform, for no reason, and to no end.

"I think, what this could boil down to finally," Lucien says. "They want us to find a haunted house."

"Yeah, it's for a kids' party," I say.

He's still holding the task sheet before his eyes, now rereading. "Find out if you're really serious," he says.

I say, "Doors, mirrors, attics, locks, hot spots."

[64]

We're at my place now. Lucien—with his shoes off, his shirt un-tucked—lying on the couch.

"Have you got," he asks, "Nintendo?"

"You can go," I tell him.

He says, "No, I was just wondering."

"I meant, you don't have to keep me company. My niece will be along any minute. Somebody's dropping her off."

"Well, thank you for your kind consideration," says Lucien. "And for letting me hang out in the air-conditioning with you for this long. I appreciate it."

"I'd rather have you *stay*," I tell him, and flick the TV back on so we can both pretend.

We gaze together at the screen as if the commercial involves more than a dull-looking twosome in fishing gear urging the purchase of something.

[65]

It's 6:30 in the A.M. Collie's opened my bedroom door a little. I see her eye.

"Where do you keep the paper cups for baking cupcakes?" she asks me.

I say, "This is Mars and we're on it."

"They're colored paper *cups*," she says.

I say, "Oh, those. They're in the drawer with my parakeets."

"Never mind," she says, and steps in and leans against a wall.

Scooting along the wall now.

I say, "You could go out and rock the porch swing off its chains."

She heaps herself onto the end of my bed as if to climb it. "What's the difference between lying and when you're making things up?" she asks.

"I know of none," I say.

"What about stories in books?"

"They don't count," I say. "They're made of writing."

[66]

• Two of my half-slips are missing,
• as well as a filing cabinet,
• a tea ball,
• the drill bits,
• my wedding album,
• the bread maker.

[67]

Adam doesn't trust banks so much anymore, or the federal government, or his consultants and accountants. He hides money in his
clothes, his books, his shoes. He takes it outside and buries it. He
won't write checks, doesn't carry plastic. He took the tags off his car!
He keeps his passport on him at all times. He mangled his driver's
license with a garden tool. He avoids phones, won't have one in his
name. He won't use electronic equipment. He despises email. He's
suspicious of machinery, technology, science, and engineering, labs,
clinics, hospitals, pharmacies, and all places involved with fitness,
health, or medicine.

[68]

"Why is Adam walking on *that* side of the wall, in the construction area?" Petal asks me.

"Because he thinks people are following him," I say.

"Like, gangster people?"

"No, I guess, more like government people."

"Aw, I don't believe that," she says. "That can't be true. Adam isn't paranoid. Are you sure you're right?"

"Positive."

"Then his brain is going," she says.

I say, "Well, yes and no. With hepatitis, you can experience—it's actually, ammonia leaking into the brain."

"You lie," says Petal.

"Never about this stuff," I say.

[69]

I'm doing this again. Here is Saunders' car, parked screwball at the end of the drive. Now his path into the house, marked by torn and dented hedges. His sunglasses, a couple of coins. The front door to the house, wide open.

Here's a shoe, inside. There's a shoe. Pieces of his clothes making a trail to the bathroom. And, at last, that'a boy, there's Saunders, down to his white undershirt, lying passed out in the sunken tub.

What could be odder than this? His body, the same as my husband's, and entirely familiar, and yet, I don't know it at all.

ONE D.O.A., ONE on the WAY

I'm scrambling in on top of him, now putting one knee on this side, the other on that, leaning to press my mouth to his throat.

He wakens. I'm shimmying my skirt up, yanking and ripping my underwear away, sliding him in and tightening around him, all as if the urge is racing ahead of me, and leaving no time for the thought, "Don't, don't," to have effect.

[70]

I'm dressed again and desperate to leave and run like crazy and get away from here. "Oh, please. You need to come to and talk to me," I'm telling Saunders.

"Why? What's a matter?"

"I just think you need to," I say.

[71]

Community Service

- 5,933 storm drains have been cleared.

- 7,151 traffic signs have been replaced.

- 9,178 streetlights have been repaired.

- 44,433 potholes have been patched.

- 95,450 trash carts have been delivered.

- 1,323,878 feet of drain lines have been cleaned.
- 18.72 million cubic yards of debris have been removed.

[72]

Lucien is late for meeting me in the Carousel Bar at The Monteleone. Same as ever, it's a piano bar with a working carousel. Truman Capote, Hemingway, Tennessee Williams. Drank themselves to vomit sick here many, many times.

[73]

I would always be late, too,

If I checked the air in all four fucking tires.

If I climbed back out of my vehicle to make certain I'd nestled the air hose securely on its arm.

If I jumped out yet another time to obtain the restroom key so I could wash my hands.

If I stood with my them under the blower until they were absolutely goddamn dry.

Or if at the parking garage, I hadn't grasped the mechanical-gate concept, that at the very fucking second the fucking stick rises, is when you go.

[74]

• Ankle Holsters are good if it's hot and you're not wearing many clothes. They're worn inside your weaker leg, with a calf strap to hold them secure.

• Pocket Holsters are molded to disguise the shape of your gun. There's a rough nap on the holster's flat side that'll supply some retention when you draw.

• Wallet Holsters, for your smallest guns, go into your back pocket. These are molded or have a dense lining so the shape of your gun won't show.

• Belly Band Holsters are on a wide elastic strip. They can hold a gun anywhere from your middle to your armpit. To stay in place, though, the band must be stretched very, very tight.

• A Belt & Slide Holster is best when you carry a big gun. This holster lets you keep your gun belted tightly to you, but outside your pants.

chapter 4

[75]

I'M WITH RHYTHM & BLUES and their parents at an eatery called The
Half Moon. Have been for every bit of an itchy hour. We're still expecting Petal.

Saunders sits across from me, tearing a crescent roll into many
parts. Adam's queasy and may be forced to bolt when they bring the
food. He has his eyes squeezed shut, his face wrinkled in a look of
rejection.

I'm in attendance but feeling as if I were sketched into the scene,
and maybe with an old pencil.

The parents sit across the table. I haven't looked up at them. Nor
will I, unless they call on me.

"I'll *have* to notify the police if those kids continue," the father
says. "They're filling the pond up with *trash*."

"What are you talking about?" asks Saunders. "Don't be fuckin'
nuts."

"The police are preoccupied these days, Father," says Adam, without opening his eyes. "They're already overwhelmed, with all they have to do."

"Like hiding under their cars," says Saunders. He brushes the remains of his crescent roll to the floor with a brisk sweep of his hand.

"Then let's hear a better suggestion," the father says to everyone. He follows himself up immediately. "I didn't suppose any of you would have one. So there's very little point in asking you at all."

"What some people are actually doing," says Adam, "is they're privately hiring off-duty police. To patrol just their particular streets."

"That's under the recently expanded definition of off-duty," says Saunders. He loosens his napkin and swats it in the air as if at a fly.

"You have to pay them, I take it," the father says.

"You do, in fact, yes," Adam says. "It is the custom to pay them their fee."

I've been shaking my head no, or nodding it yes.

Saunders has wrapped his napkin like a bandage around his forearm. He's trying to tuck the napkin's corner tail in with his teeth.

Adam rouses, lifts my wrist and checks it for a watch.

His father scowls and asks, "What the hell damn difference does it make, what time it is?"

"It's O.K.," Adam gestures with his hand.

The sunset ignites the west windows.

These four are making me want to die.

Over there, the father, preparing to drink his espresso, makes a little music with his cup and silver spoon.

[76]

Petal appears up front in the welcoming bay, dressed in an ivory blouse and black suit. Saunders rises from his chair, and saunters up to escort her.

He doesn't return with her, though. The two linger there in the bay.

I see some of it. It's an argument they're having. Petal is, anyway, arguing.

"Chill" is too narrow a word for what passes over me, and it describes only part of the experience.

Petal has ripped her pearl necklace off her throat and is whipping it at Saunders.

"What the hell are they doing?" the father asks. "What's the hold up? Can anyone see?"

From out on the street comes an outburst of music. Someone is improvising with a horn.

"Adam!" the father says, and leans over the table to tag his son's arm. "Give me an explanation for this. I want to know what's going on."

"Petal seems angry," Adam says.

I am very barely breathing.

Up there now, Petal's tearing at her blouse, wrenching off a button, and flinging that at Saunders.

Her hair was pinned up when she entered, but she's dismissed whatever pins and combs held it that way.

"I can see her brassiere!" says the father. "Goddamn it. Adam! Goddamn it to hell. You get up there immediately and put a stop to this."

"Uh unh," Adam says, "not for a wad of money."

[77]

Saunders and Petal have left. Adam and his parents are leaving.

The mother comes around on her way past and leans over my left ear. She says, "Let's be careful to keep both feet planted firmly in reality."

"Yeah, O.K. Good plan," I say.

She says, "You don't have to accept as whole-cloth truth everything that passes before your eyes, now do you?"

I'm not smart enough to answer her. It'll take two days minimum to prepare a response.

[78]

I'm lollygagging at the table here. There's no hurry, and no one's expecting me. My husband's gone to one place, I'll be going to another.

I've forked up my lemon crème brûlée while allowing those who have gone out ahead of me to get very far, far away.

[79]

This is Saunders' Benz, at the edge of the dimly lighted lot.

And, that is Saunders himself in rubbery drape over the steering wheel. His face tilted up. His mouth slightly open.

I'm at the window, and this is Petal in the passenger seat, pointing at Saunders with a long black gun.

"Oh holy God, no," I say, "Holy, holy God."

"He's all right," Petal says. "The son of bitch passed out. Because he insisted on some last swigs of tequila before he died. I should have known."

"At least you didn't shoot him."

"Stick around," Petal says.

I open the door on her side and take her by the shoulder. "We have to go now, O.K.? We really have to go. He'll wake up sitting here. Maybe won't even remember. He could draw a total blank and think nothing happened at all."

"Very little did," she says as she lifts out.

She bumps the car door shut behind her. Standing here in her shredded blouse, her hair fallen out of its coif.

"Better let me carry the gun," I say.

[80]

We're driving alongside an aboveground cemetery—a vast and gleaming village of graves. Brilliant lawns, lighted up for the handful of parishioners going in and out of a tiny chapel with a peacock-blue roof.

I say, "I think it's, you know, hospital time."

"Don't fool around with me," Petal says.

"That's what we're doing, we're not fooling around."

"You mean a mental facility? Lucky for me there aren't any; they all went down in the flood."

I look over, and she's staring straight ahead, her fists, one on each thigh, clenched to knots. So beautiful and so every bit backward.

I say, "Well, there's one left, that I know. Saint Antoine's, in Jefferson Parish. It's not particularly nice digs. And it'll cost you a bucket of money."

"I can't wait," Petal says.

"It'll have to do, though, because think about it. If Saunders does remember anything? If sometime, anytime, he ever mentions the word gun to his parents?"

A sigh from her.

I say, "This way, here's how I'll put it. She's taking the necessary steps. In a very positive direction. That was a low, but she's now on the upswing. She's given herself over to professionals for guidance."

"Glory," says Petal. "Listen to all the slogans and crap in your head."

[81]

We're in a tunnel of trees now, on a little road at the entryway of St. Antoine's.

There's a warm fog in the air and under the gigantic trees, great streams of fog ahead in the lights around the main building, fog on Petal's face and in her hair.

She's getting herself ready, fastening her poor blouse together with safety pins.

[82]

A Place Called Home

- There remain an estimated 80,000 vacant dwellings.
- The costs of insurance and building materials have spiraled.
- 86,000 families still inhabit FEMA trailers.
- 94 percent of the trailers have formaldehyde levels that are 75 times the recommended maximum.

[83]

On the ride back from the hospital, I let the radio do the talking. A man on there is telling me: "Nice sharp anvil pruners. You'll need one for the woody stems. And, of course, a bypass pruner. Also, your lopping shears."

It's getting light. I'm driving on a concrete bridge over a valley of kudzu that blankets the land from here to the horizon. There's a line of kudzu-covered trees, like a march of great misshapen animals.

Seen a different way, what I just conducted was the confinement of my lover's wife.

And that I'm now speeding away and in possession of her loaded firearm.

[84]

There has always seemed something more going on with Petal. When she's stuck smiling, and can't unload the smile. Or when she's not answering. Or, she's answering, but not at the correct rate. Saying something too quickly, or saying it much later, when it's all but pointless to say.

High on her left cheekbone, she has a scar that's a delicate crescent. I've never asked her the origin. My guess is an accident long ago. But not having the scar erased, that was a smart bit of business. It cozens and appeases people, the existence of a flaw on that exquisite face.

[85]

Lucien phones in the A.M. "What about work?" he asks me.

I say, "Oh, fuck work. There's no real work. You mean photographing some woman's house?"

"That's," he says, "correct at what I'm referring to."

I roll off the bed and start pounding around the room. "Well, I'm not doing it," I say. "I'm sleeping through this part of my life that has nothing and no real work in it."

"What that does, though," Lucien says, "is force me to take all the pictures myself. No problem. You are assured. But, if it is the woman's house, what there is to tell her, I do not know. Or, her and her husband, if the case may be."

On my silent TV's screen there's a funnel cloud twirling with a whole trailer home inside it. Hail the size of nectarines.

"You'll be fine," I say.

There I am in the mirror—a pale and messed-up woman making a further mess in the messed-up world.

He says, "Suppose they begin to pressure me."

"Lie. Make something up," I say. "Tell them whatever comes into your head."

"But what if they need an answer?"

"Lie."

He says, "Well, I guess, thank you."

"Happy to be of help," I say.

[86]

Nineteen seconds and I'm calling him back. "Here's what you do. Are you ready? Park where you can see everything, and climb onto the hood. Take wide-angle shots. Then closer in, medium shots. Next, get inside the front doors of the house and shoot facing out. Go behind the place, do the same thing. Back inside, turn on all the lights. Shoot only the largest rooms, from one corner, then the opposite. Get the doorways. Do tight shots of the ceilings, built-in bookcase or fireplace. Now outside, shoot through the windows and from the terrace."

"I can do that, if that's all."

"Gosh, no," I say. "You get the gate, the pergola, the grounds-keeper's. Then right before sunset, do all the outside shots again."

[87]

I'm cruising up to Petal's house. It's a slender two-story—brick, blue shutters, the facade trimmed with West Indian ivy. The place is quiet. The walkway's all tidy and quiet. I see no Saunders' stuff strewn around.

I have to get up the nerve to go inside there and fetch Petal's personal things.

I'm turning in, creeping in my car up the driveway, where, on this particular scorching-hot day, I'll sit and try to work up the nerve.

[88]

Saunders is here. He's on a divan in the dark front parlor, alone, drinking straight from a bottle of rum.

I go in and sit beside him. I say, "Looks like you've been doing a lot of thinking."

He puts his hand on my face. "I want to know where my wife is," he says.

I haven't quite finished the editing on what I'm going to tell him, and how to explain everything that has happened, briefly, and with most of what happened left out.

Saunders is moodier, more complicated than Adam. Sometimes, rather than get confused, he'll become very literal, and very exacting about times and specifics. He'll want to go back over and over a thing, back over the chronology, and the sequence in which things occurred.

This could trip me up.

I say, "Petal was ready to shoot you in the heart, so I seized her weapon, and drove her to a psychiatric hospital to get treatment. That's where she is, at the moment."

"Ha, ha. Very funny," he says.

"No, baby," I say.

"Then you mean for real."

"Well, I do. Yes. It's what we're dealing with. The situation."

"Is that right." He drinks from the bottle, an amount that balloons his cheeks.

"Leave some for me," I say. "Unless you're too angry."

He swallows and leans back, staring at me or through me, or at someone who's not here, at what she's done, or he's done, or what we.

[89]

One Will Be Appointed for You Free of Charge

• The funding for the Indigent-Defender System is traffic ticket revenue.

• Traffic ticket revenue has all but dried up.

• There have been as few as 6 public defenders.

• An Orleans judge wrote to 450 lawyers and demanded they do pro bono work in Criminal Court. They declined.

"We've still got three more things to scavenge," says Lucien, and settles into the passenger's seat.

"Aw damn it, I was afraid of that," I say.

He sucks in his stomach and draws a folded piece of paper from his pants' pocket.

Lucien's wearing his glasses today, I notice. They ride on his nose and he looks over them at everything. They are apparently useless for seeing through.

The page he's unfolding has its corner chewed off. "Did one of your dogs attack that?" I ask.

"Uh, I can't have dogs," he says. "I can't take care of them." He reads to me aloud from the sheet: "A hat-check place. A beauty parlor with a woman's name. Those are the two biggest items on here before we're done."

"What became of your dogs? Did something happen? I thought you told me you had seven dogs."

"I've just got Billy," he says.

"You have no dogs, except you have Billy?"

He nods, which seems an incomplete, unsatisfying answer.

But I'm firing the engine and backing out the van. This is one of the specifics in Lucien's life that I needn't know much about. "Well, you can't always tell with dogs," I say. "Whether they're coming or going."

[91]

"I'm asleep," I tell Collie as she creeps around my room.

"I'm making cinnamon toast," she says.

"Is that something you're allowed to do?"

"No, I'm making cinnamon toast for our *breakfast*."

"At my house, you are never, ever permitted to cook at my house ever. Were you older, I'd ask you to make coffee. You wouldn't have to fuss around with a cup or anything, but just bring me the whole carafe."

Missing are:

- my caulking gun,
- the clock radio,
- a pair of espadrilles,
- my framed Tulane degree,
- a nutcracker,
- my raincoat.

[92]

Adam's been asleep for a very long while. I just sit here, because, I don't know.

What a pre-fucking-posterous disease! He doesn't show symptoms. He doesn't, he told me once, "experience disease progression." It's the meds, in my view, making him sleep.

Certainly is a lovely bedroom, that he has. White Egyptian cotton on the pillows and on the bed. A blue crystal drinking glass on the nightstand.

"Bubba," I say as he's waking.

"Yeah," he says, and lifts onto his elbows. His eyes are lowered and not fixed on anything.

I ask, "Why don't they just be done with this nonsense? It's conking you out for hours on end. They should either halt the meds or sock you into the hospital."

"No," he says, and flops onto his back again.

"No, what?"

"No go. No hospital. They don't have beds for stuff like that. Don't you ever watch the news? If my liver were to fall out, splat, they might put me on a waiting list for a hospital bed. But even then, they'd only do it because I'm one of the handful who's got health insurance."

"Then what about going off the treatment? Because it doesn't appear to have been a success," I say.

"Yes, actually, I'm about at the point where they recommend stopping. Of course, that exhausts the medical therapies, you understand."

"Not entirely sure I do."

"There's nothing else," he says, "in the doctor kit."

[93]

The father's sitting alone down here in a shadowy parlor where the wallpaper looks like the palest pink silk.

"Why," I ask him, "is no one doing anything? Could somebody tell me?"

"The government?" he asks.

"I won't answer no to that. But, right now my focus is on Adam."

He flaps his folded newspaper page lightly on his thigh, exhales tiredly. "You have no right, and no grounds, to question the care and treatment my son's been getting."

I say, "It seems like a long gray line, to me. He never improves. Not one squinch. He just goes on and on, being dreadfully sick. How do you explain that?"

The father makes a pointed shape with his index fingers. "What I'm hearing, frankly, is an indication of a need," he says, "for more knowledge and information on your part."

"Say again?"

He lets a second or two tick by. He says, "Quite a lot has been written about this disease. Volumes and volumes. I don't have the time or the inclination to sit here now and familiarize you with all of it."

I lean back on my shoes, let my gaze wander the interior architecture—movements meant to convey that I have no desire for further conversation.

[94]

The temperature has dropped below eighty-five, so my windows are
open, and there's a breeze carrying in smells of molasses, oranges,
chicory, papayas, camellias, rum, sorghum, powdered sugar, gum-
bo, newspapers, dogs, road tar, cigars, garbage, etouffée, perfumed
women, babies, lumber, jambalaya, sex, car exhaust, saltwater, bourbon, horses, manure, coffee, absinthe, roses, seafood, urine, Tabasco,
crawfish, prostitutes, lemonade, barbecue, pianos, sweat, the river,
bananas.

[95]

Adam's is the chronic kind of Hepatitis C. A percentage of those
inflicted are cleared of it with medication, but most are not. I must
never borrow his razor, must never use his toothbrush by mistake.
Otherwise, nothing's going to jump onto me.

Only my second day at the library and I'm already tired of reading this stuff. Although, there is more.

[96]

- OWB Holsters (Outside-the-Waistband) ride close to your
  body, just behind your hip bone. You cover them with a
  jacket or an untucked shirt.

- IWB Holsters (Inside-the-Waistband) clip onto your belt
  and hold the gun next to you, inside your pants.

- Groin Holsters, for example, stay under your waistband, and once in place, don't restrict your movements at all.

- A Shoulder Holster is the best choice when driving your vehicle, as your seatbelt and harness could, with another holster, cause delays in getting to your gun.

⌈97⌉

Lucien's searching in his backpack for a panoramic lens. He says, "It's in here, *believe* me. There's a bunch of things down inside here, if you know where to look. You've just got to be willing to hunt. Too, you have to know exactly what you're looking for, although, it might not be worth it."

I'm ignoring him, busy at an intersection, noting that every other car gets to go first a couple times.

⌈98⌉

The causeway over Lake Pontchartrain is the number one longest bridge in the world. Nevertheless, we drive on it for twenty-four minutes, headed over to Mandeville to run some errand for our employer.

"If you think this is bad," I say to Lucien.

"I'm good," he says.

"Well, I'll tell you anyway. When they used to cross the Lake in their paddlewheel boats or what boats they had, it would take them five and a half hours."

"Whew, then I guess we are blessed," he says.

I say, "It must've sounded like I was implying that."

"Were you not?"

"Oh," I say, "sure. Consciously or un."

But I'm going to stop talking now and from here on be more careful, as I would rather drink kerosene than suggest that a local have gratitude.

[99]

The Northshore is choking with people and companies and businesses that have relocated over here. They've bought everything. The shops are gutted, the shelves cleared. What little is left costs seventy-nine times what it's supposed to.

[100]

"Hold me closer, tiny dancer," sing the patrons of the drywall store.

[101]

Here in the grocery, a customer has found an intact package of cinnamon buns.

"I can pay for mine," he assures his companion.

[102]

Health and Well-Being

- An estimated 4,486 New Orleans physicians fled the storm.

- The Journal of the AMA found only 17 psychiatrists returned to the city—that's 1 per 16,058.

- The suicide rate post-Katrina rose almost 300 percent.

- Charity Hospital, which provided all medical care for the city's poor, has closed its doors forever.

[103]

"Another group with a sizeable income," says one of my seatmates here in the mental hospital's Visitor's Lounge. "The air traffic controllers. They are paid almost as handsomely as the pilots themselves, and do you know those scalawags make nearly as much as the oral surgeons and the anesthesiologists."

Another visitor says, "All right, I admit it. I'm aching to hear who's in the lowest-income column."

"That is a fairly predictable listing, I'm afraid. The exceptions being the professions we simply aren't well aware of—the dog shampooers, for example, or the members of a ski patrol. Personally, I was surprised to find that the greenhouse workers have a particularly low income average."

"And, the very lowest?" asks visitor two.

"According to the data, the *lowest*-lowest is, lamentably, the coffee shop hostess."

The second visitor gives and airy sigh. "I am sad to hear that. That is troubling. Very, very sad."

[104]

This lounge has a rug, a couple lamp tables, a half-dozen chairs, no windows. The air conditioner is working, but not very hard.

Petal's face is squashed flat on her palm and she watches me through a thick lens of the drugs that have been given her.

"So, how've you been? What's been going on?" I ask.

Because people are morons, including me.

"Ah, let's see. We went for a group walk—lined up two by two. They had us choose partners."

"That sounds O.K."

"Ah, no," she says. "Mine started crying right away. Really, a bunch of them started crying."

"How come?"

She sighs.

"General," I say, "type of crying."

"All right, leave it," she says.

"This is bad. This is dismal," I tell her, unable to go on pretending any other attitude. "I'm so sorry you're here. I'm sorry I am."

She coughs and says, "There's mould in the rooms. I hope to hell all I have is tuberculosis."

I say, "You know, up until later on today, I never really knew how to drink."

[105]

The air has a damp, agitated quality tonight and it's carrying voices and saxophone music and a million other sounds.

My streetcar is already moving. I'm sitting by an open window, trying to think.

Past cafes, and sherbet-colored cottages, white churches, and cobblestone streets, brick row-houses, their balconies roped with tea lights and draped with ferns.

Here's a man carrying a wire birdcage.

New Orleans is full of meanings I haven't learned. I've had many of them explained to me but the words didn't get through. I still don't understand.

chapter 5

[106]

- I'm never again calling my congressperson and screaming "Liar!" into the phone.
- I'm never again eating a Slim Jim.
- I've snapped another person with my bra for the last time.
- Diving from a height onto packaging peanuts is over.
- So are any communications written in lipstick on my chest.

[107]

It's hot here tonight in City Park by the lighted clay tennis courts where Saunders is playing his dad. There are the predictable sounds coming from them—groaning, swearing, argument, and hurrah.

Adam's lounging beside me on a bench, smoking a dark little cigar. We're neither of us paying any attention to the game. Adam isn't, for his reasons; I'm not, for mine.

These Live Oak trees, melodramatically draped, it seems to me, are six or so hundred years old.

"You want to go to Lilette later or afterward, or where do you want to go?" I ask the husband.

"Lilette?" he says.

"You've been there countless times. Where you have the crawfish pies. It's got white leather booths?"

"Oh, you mean the one by your place. Our place. Your place, if that's what you'd prefer."

I say, "No. Adam. You paid for it, and it's still got plenty of your—"

"Fecal matter," he says with a nod and a sigh.

[108]

"You're not sending me out like a sheep among production people, are you? I do not feel prepared to conversate with them."

"Tell them," I say, "that we're exceedingly conscientious with budgets and schedules."

He raises an eyebrow to ask if that's true.

I say, "Change the word 'conscientious' if it makes you uncomfortable."

"It doesn't you?"

"Uh, no. Or very rarely," I say. "All right, tell them we're exceedingly *diligent* with budgets and schedules."

His eyes are lowered and he's not really looking at me, but with his gaze fixed around my collarbone and throat.

I say, "O.K. We are exceedingly attentive to . . ."

Now he looks at me.

"Strike exceedingly, if you're going to be a baby. We are attentive, and we'll remain attentive. To their every fucking moment and dime!"

[109]

The neighbor kids are outside the parents' place again, messing around by the pond.

I watched them through the windows earlier, catcalling and lobbing things over the fence—water balloons and a volleyball, sure. I can understand throwing those. Then a pair of high-heeled shoes I wouldn't have predicted. A few ears of corn. A tricycle. They're definitely headed for trouble, those kids. Now it's bananas.

"That's it. I've had enough. It's time to inform the police," says the father.

"Nah," says Saunders, "it isn't."

"Maybe you could just find out what school they go to," I say. Saunders and his father glare at me.

"And, you know, report them."

"That could work. Listen to her. That really might solve it," says Saunders.

The father says, "School authorities can't handle the likes of these kids. Don't be so naïve. The police are the only ones equipped to do so."

"Let me insert something," says Saunders, whom I now think is Adam. "You don't do that. You don't call the police. Ever. Never summon the police."

That's Saunders. It has to be.

"I want your word on this, Father," he says.

"I'm not giving you my word!"

"You are so. Otherwise, we're all at risk."

Adam, I'm thinking now. Whichever. I say to the dad, "He means the police won't respond anyway. They'll utterly ignore your complaint. But they might write down the address and note that you're a bad troublemaker."

"You people!" the father says. "It's like you live in fear of the *Federales* descending. That's exactly how it sounds!"

"Well," I say, "then, let it," and the twin motions for the father to zip his lip.

[110]

Upstairs here, the sitting rooms have twirling fans, thick carpets, enormous vases of pampas grass. There are overstuffed easy chairs, blue and yellow ceramics.

I'm on a sofa, involved in hating my in-laws for their wealth. I hate them also when I'm washing up. In their bathrooms are sunken stone tubs, linen rugs from Portugal, copper fixtures, mosaic floor tiles, lemon trees in turquoise Bauer Jardinières.

There's an oval library downstairs, and a salon painted dove gray where sits an Astin-Weight baby grand piano. In the parlors are benches covered in quilted silk, Meissen porcelains, black-and-white photography, Italian chairs with embroidered seat cushions.

When I'm down there, my hatred can make me feel faint. Someday, it'll knock me unconscious.

[111]

At the Camellia Grill, someone behind me says, "Their crawfish is better than you might expect."

I'm dining alone, so I look around, maybe see if this guy can be trusted. He's at a table at about four o'clock, if I were the center of the timepiece. He's wearing a t-shirt printed with the words CEMENT SYSTEMS. I don't know what the hell that could be. So, no, pay attention to nothing he utters.

[112]

"I can deal with a lot, but *not*," Lucien says, and with four jerks of the head, sings: "Hot, child, in the, city."

He's anxiously checking his different pockets, hunting for something, possibly. "Keys?" he asks, and answers, "Yes. Lint all over me? Yes, got plenty."

[113]

"Mind if I watch TV?" he asks later, at my place.

"Can if you want to, but I already looked," I say, "and *Dog the Bounty Hunter* is the best thing on."

He's flipping channels with a small bit of urgency. "I'm buying something from a shopping network," he says, and settles back into the furniture.

He lifts and exercises an ankle.

He says, "Before you ask me—"

"I wasn't going to!" I tell him. "I wouldn't! Ever! I won't!"

[114]

Among the things I cannot find are:

- the basting brush,
- the clothes hamper,
- my bedroom slippers,
- a black lace push-up bra,

- the glue gun,

- the entire sewing machine.

[115]

A few hours ago, I woke up with Saunders in bed next to me. He was sitting with his back against the metal headboard, shirtless, in unzipped jeans, chain-smoking and staring off, and listening, I suppose, to the piano music coming from outside.

This was like a dream, though not an actual dream, but with dream features abounding. A bird flew in and back out the window. A strip of silver cloth was knotted around my ankle. I've never before seen Saunders smoke. It was raining outside but no, it wasn't.

[116]

Family Values

- The homeless population has almost doubled.

- 80 percent of New Orleans public housing remains closed, and 5000 public units are slated for, or are under demolition.

- Public transportation has been cut by two-thirds.

- Fewer than 50 percent of the schools have reopened. Children are put on waiting lists to attend.

- The only high school in the Lower 9th Ward, Alfred Lawless, is not scheduled to reopen ever.

- Louisiana finished dead last in the Health Index for the past three years running.

[117]

I came in this afternoon to the offices of the agency that employs me and took a seat at an empty desk in the middle of everyone. My co-workers adjusted themselves for a look at me.

Now they're all looking away. It's as if I've dissolved and there's nothing to see anymore. But that's all right. I get it. Everything's O.K. I *work* for this agency, while they come in every day and work *here*.

Someone calls out, "Be sure Gerald's aware," and someone else says, "Chris, I told you I'm already on it."

I'm writing nonsense in my check register for something to do, or to look like something I'm doing. Now a wish list of songs to find on the World Wide Web and put on my MP3 player—Peggy Lee doing "Don't Smoke in Bed." Anything by Lena Horne. Louis Armstrong, naturally.

A conversation has been going on behind me. Or, more like a talk. "It's not all that mystifying," one man is saying. "First, you had the switch from revolvers, which hold six rounds, to semiautomatic pistols, which hold ten. Next, the switch to higher *calibers*, from .22s and .38s to your 9-millimeters and 40-calibers. Then you started seeing Pocket Rockets—that're lightweight, very deadly, and hiding them is easy as could be. But I'm happy enough with what I got. A Ruger, a Taurus, a Beretta."

"Which Taurus?" asks a second man.

"The Pro Forty-Five," says the first.

"*Knew* you were going to say that.

"I also," says the first man, "like very, very much the Stoeger Cougar."

[118]

I need a cane field for a local car-dealer ad.

"Where is it we're *going*?" asks Lucien, in the back of the van. He's lying on the seat, feeling queasy. "Too bumpy!" he says.

I say, "We're looking for cane."

I'm speeding out on the Great River Road, which doesn't run in a steady strip alongside the Mississippi, but as dozens of little rural roads strung together. You can't even see the river. It's over there, beyond the levee and the batture.

There are loud-colored Creole cottages, bayous studded with red maples and mangroves, oil wells, tank farms, cemeteries, fields and fields of sugarcane.

The van buckets over some maw in the pavement and Lucien groans.

"My apologies," I say. "It's not me, it's this road."

"It's my fault anyway," he tells me. "I stayed out too late."

"Where'd you go?"

"Galatoire's," he says.

"Alone?"

He says, "No, of course, not. My grandma took me with her money that she won at the casino. You know what she plays? What she always plays? That gargantuan *wheel.*"

He says, "Two people. But we ate a hundred eighty dollars worth of food."

[119]

"I'm fast at this game," Lucien says from across the room.

"That you are!" I say, without looking up, because being supportive is preferable to asking what game he's talking about. He'd answer in full, and it still wouldn't make any sense to me.

[120]

"Where were you so long?" I ask as Petal moseys out and joins me in the visitors' area.

"Card game," she says, showing me a little wad of bills.

Overhead here are the branches of a pomegranate tree. A squirrel or whatever just kicked a nut down on me. Or, perhaps that was an accident.

[121]

Attention to What's Going On Around You

• pointy metal furniture,

• not enough cushions,

• top of the day heat,

• a woman with her mouth open, lying on a gurney,

• a fire of paper and cigarettes atop one of the metal urns,

• hillshit guys, lying and bragging about their achievements,

• sounds from all the berserk children who were miserably dragged here.

[122]

Adam is in his sitting room, in an easy chair, watching a History Channel biography of General George Custer, and having martinis served, glass after glass.

Saunders is here too, pacing back and forth, and speaking emphatically into his cell phone: "This is all in the past tense, you dig? The bill for booking him was already seventy-five thousand dollars."

They are both wearing khaki shorts that look heartbreakingly beautiful on both of them.

"No, it is not right. You know it's not right," Saunders says into the phone.

"Certainly, you may," he says, before clicking off. He walks angrily around in a tight circle.

"Can we stop now?" Adam asks him.

I don't know what they're talking about and haggling over—an event that, were I invited, I would probably blow off. Still, I'm listening and nodding at each of them in turn.

"Seriously. Haven't we exhausted this?" asks Adam.

Saunders says, "I don't see that you've done anything, other than sit there."

"Ah, you forget I'm the one who paid."

"Aw, fuck you, like you'd let me forget."

"Don't you swear at him, Saunders," I say.

"Don't you swear at him, Saunders," he repeats, in a voice that actually is eerily similar to mine.

"People, people," says Adam.

[123]

"Go up again, one," Saunders says. "Isn't that *Breathless?* The Goddard movie?"

"And not 'Breathless' the talk show," Adam says. "Yes, it's Jean Seberg."

He stamps the TV remote down on his nightstand. And what a handsome little yellow-lacquered antique it is. He's sitting on the bed with his legs crossed now, his folded hands resting on his ankles. He says, "You know, the CIA really drove that girl to suicide."

"Well," Saunders says, and pauses to finish his drink before his sentence. "In fairness to the CIA, they do kind of *admit* they did that."

"Look," he says, taking up control of the remote. "Prescription drugs that can make a wife have passion."

I say, "Another simpler way for her would be, marry a man you're attracted to!"

Saunders inhales deeply and turns his whole torso my way. "In a marriage," he begins.

"Yes?" I say. "I am listening."

[124]

I'm having Collie sort through a heap of my stuff that she has in her room.

"This was a present," she's saying. "This one's mine, from home. These in this corner, I bought at a store."

"Oh, you did, did you?"

"Yes," she says. " You can ask my dad and mom."

She's wearing a hot pink turtleneck, and on her little legs, vivid violet tights.

"So, you don't think we need to go through those one-by-one? To make sure?" I ask.

"I don't think we have to." Now using her whole body to try to shake open the door.

I say, "Well, I think we do. So I'll sit here and wait. I'm capable of waiting for a very-very long-long time."

[125]

Lucien says, "I dreamed I was boycotting Wal-Mart," and nods to himself. "That just came back to me."

"Only a dream," I remind him.

[126]

I say, "Our work, if we ever have any again, is in Pre-Production and it ordinarily stops when filming begins. We're merely setting things up for the Locations Department.

"Say, they need an office building that looks like the nineteen forties in Wichita, Kansas. So, fine, we find that. But, this has to be a building that can be accessed by crews and trucks and equipment. Someplace everybody can get to on time, from hotels and possibly from the airport. Then we negotiate if the building can be available, and can take a break from its business, if need be—so there won't be people shuffling in and out—and if it could be rented for a price within reason. Now, all we've got left is the practical stuff. Parking. Parking for grips, for construction, lighting, camera, sound. Then also for catering, wardrobe, offices, restrooms, trash, so on and so forth. Blocking the streets around the building. Can we get a permit for those streets? Cops to do that, and more cops for traffic. Bearing in mind they're like forty bucks an hour each, with a minimum of four hours. So, just how many of these cops can we really afford?

"Or, suppose we learn, suddenly—which we should have investigated first thing, but we neglected to—that we're right smack dab in a hospital's flight path for their helicopters. Obviously, they can't hold off and keep quiet during filming."

"What do we do?"

"Nothing," I say, and shrug. "Start the fuck over."

[127]

- Ankle Holsters keep your smaller guns very well concealed. However, getting the pants' leg up and getting the gun drawn might prove awkward.

- Small-of-the-Back Holsters are the most easily concealed, but they are not at all comfortable for sitting, and drawing from one can be both clumsy and dangerously time-consuming.

- Strong-Side Holsters allow you to draw your gun rapidly and, in most situations, with more ease than any other holster.

- Cross-Draw Holsters are worn on the left side, over the trouser pocket, and close to the body. Note that a gun drawn from a Cross-Draw holster will be pointed behind you, and unless you're careful this could result in a problem.

[128]

You take a picture. It doesn't have to be very good, believe me. You'll make it good in the editing. Something is about to happen. Don't think about that too hard. Open Photoshop. Deepen the shadows and highlights. Add to the shadows. Add to the light. Sharpen the contrast.

chapter 6

[129]

In the Criminal Justice System

- 88 percent of the murder cases in New Orleans result in acquittal.

- Police officers can't be taken off their assignments to testify in court.

- 3,581 suspects, many charged with murder, walked free in '07 when the prosecutor's office failed to gather evidence in time.

- The District Attorney resigned the same year at the insistence of the mayor. The State Attorney resigned.

- The rate of Armed Robbery is up 1,022 percent.

- The per capita Homicide Rate is now 15 times higher than that of New York City.

[130]

"Explain to me," I say to my husband.

"No, come on," he says to me. "Don't."

I'm at the window. My back to him. One hundred thousand arguments have dead-ended just so, with the male in the argument refusing to do a thing and withholding information.

"Why aren't you at work?" he asks me.

"Because, there *isn't* any more," I say. "Because work's over."

[131]

"This is just . . ." I hear him saying in his sleep in the night, "it's just pain."

[132]

We're out in a little rental boat on one of the lagoons that used to be Bayou Metairie, Lucien and I. Nothing else on the water but a duck or two and a lone goose. There's a canopy of cypress trees and six-hundred-year-old Live Oaks, their branches so draped with moss they touch the ground.

"Have you ever heard of that 'One Ton Tree' program?" Lucien asks. "It's a thing to get a lot of trees planted in a hurry."

"Ah, because of the toxins in the soil. I read that the flooding elevated toxins all over town."

"Well, yeah," he says. "Because it killed fifty thousand trees. Then, despite that, you'll hear different people telling you that things were always horrible, so nothing else is new."

"This can rub me raw," he says. "It's really just commanding you to shut up."

"It's homogenizing."

"It's homogenizing," Lucien repeats. "That's it exactly. It's like nobody suffered. Nobody is struggling. Not compared to what was."

"There are precedents," I say.

"They're nothing either, it turns out!"

I say, "I get it. The Great Depression was merely one in a series of depressions."

"Right, so, if you're depressed now, don't cry about it. 'Cause there never was a time when you weren't depressed."

"Well, that particular argument has some merit," I say.

[133]

"What about Tippetina's?" asks Adam. "We never go there. We haven't been there since James Brown."

"I have, actually," I say.

"Haven't," says Saunders. "You couldn't go without us."

"I imagine she's mistaking the place," Adam says.

"No, I'm not."

He says, "Saunders? Trust me. She's confusing it with someplace else."

"No," I say, "I'm not. How could I confuse Tippetina's?"

"All right, then with whom did you go? Because you didn't go alone," Adam says.

I say, "Men of the Grip Truck."

"You shouldn't be suggesting about going out to a club," Saunders says.

"Yes, you shouldn't, Adam," I say, "while Saunders' wife is, uh, away."

"I hadn't even thought of that," Saunders says. "Though it's hideous and a principle reason for us not to go out. I meant he shouldn't because he'll die if he drinks! He has a fucking liver disease. How deep in denial are you people?"

"I try not to think about it," Adam says.

"Yeah," I say, "I try not to think about it."

"Then somebody damn well better," says Saunders.

"Thanks," Adam says.

"From me too, Saunders, thanks."

I say, "I really mean that. Deeply appreciate it. And, just to show you, in return, I'll be the one to remember about your wife."

[134]

Here's a fellow in rimless glasses, talking to a curly-haired woman, demanding to know from her, "All right, *who?*"

Now a guy in a squash-gold uniform running furiously and with his arms spread to move people out of the way.

Papaya trees in an abandoned lot, their limbs sagging with rotted fruit.

Now at the corner, a couple of female office workers, tugging at their waistlines and comparing how many pounds they've each lost.

[135]

I thought this guy in the diner looked a little jarred and now he's got a gun out on the table. "You want to fuck with me?" he asks over and over, as he's turning the gun to point at this diner or that. Not at me, yet.

There's another fellow at a table between the bad guy and me, and he's gone right on drinking coffee and eating a madeleine.

The gun guy, he has a long head, long face, a short-sleeved shirt, bleached hair. Now he turns the gun at someone and says, "You're it." Turns it to someone else, "Now, you're it."

"Do you want to fuck with me?" he's yelling, but he needn't; it's not like the rest of us are making a lot of noise.

[136]

Petal ticks the ash from her cigarette and stares at the glowing end.

We're sitting on the iron furniture outside the hospital. There are strings of lights winking and blinking over the banks of daffodils and agapanthus.

"Forgive me if I mistook," I say. "You were aiming it right at his chest, remember?"

She drops her cigarette and stamps it into the ground, saying, "I need an ashtray. In addition to this area around my feet here, which is full."

She says, "Yes, I remember. Certainly do remember."

[137]

Lucien and I wander upstairs in the twins' parents' house, looking for anyone home.

Here's Saunders, finally, in the cool of the library, seated among the gleaming wooden shelves. He leaps from his armchair as we approach. He removes and pockets his eyeglasses.

"You haven't met Lucien," I say.

Saunders, extending his hand, says, "I've wanted to for so long. At last. Wonderful. At last."

"I'm just her intern," says Lucien. "I *did* actually talk to you guys once before."

I say, "Yes, we were all at an auction together. Over in Metairie. Lucien and I, and you twins, Hammer and Tongs. But I didn't get a chance to do the introductions then."

"Well, you've made up for that now. Hallelujah!" says Saunders.

"Another time," Lucien says, "I spoke to you, I'm pretty sure, when I called here by mistake."

"Oh, right. From jail! Now that must have been something," Saunders says.

"No, it was just from my grandma's house," Lucien says. "Only you or your other twin told me nobody else was home. Which, why would you have lied about it?"

"I'll answer that," I say. "This one's mine."

[138]

Everyday Life

• The water system is ravaged and it's losing 50 million gallons of water every day.

• The sewage system too is near collapse.

• New Orleans East, Gentilly, and the Lower 9th Ward, remain almost uninhabited.

• The "X" and the grim notations that were spray-painted by Search & Rescue teams still adorn numberless houses.

[139]

Lucien says, "They mean twelve million, right?"

I say, "No, twelve million wouldn't buy anything. Twelve *billion* to build Force-Five Dykes along the coast."

"That's a lot of jack," says he.

"Alternatively, one hundred twenty-five billion, and counting," Adam says, "for cleanup and repair."

Lucien isn't coming off all that well in this conversation with my husband. Never the fucking less, it's a conversation, and they're having it.

[140]

I'm saying, "A three-story parking garage. One that would provide enough space for camera trucks, catering wagons, production vans. Plus secure warehouse space for all the set decoration and props."

"This is *just* what they have in Shreveport," says Lucien.

"Well, theirs is good, yeah. Shreveport's is good. But it's a hundred-thousand square feet. This is three-hundred-twenty thousand. This is a nine-block-long film studio. With sound stages, post-production facilities. Besides that, it's a training center for every skill—crew school, essentially. Crew school and a film studio."

"This is the thing near Tremé?" Adam asks me.

"Near Tremé," I say. "And for the economy, this is like getting an auto plant in here. Consider. About half a movie's budget is spent in state. Half of that for salaries, and the other goes to food, housing, construction. That's very big money poured directly in."

I say, "There're the hundreds of crew and office workers—carpenters, accountants, electricians, transportation. Hundreds more hired as extras. Hotels, catering, dry-cleaning. The stores they shop at, the restaurants where they eat. Galleries. They buy art, they buy furniture, accessories. Paint. The paint they buy for scenery on a single film can cost ten thousand dollars."

Lucien says, "I think it was for '06, Shreveport took in three hundred million."

I say, "Yeah, and wasn't that gallant of them to step up?"

"You're lucky they didn't decide to film in another state," says Adam.

"Well, that's me, yep, so lucky."

"You know this," he says to me. "The tax credits aren't going to continue to draw people. Not when you have thirty other states starting to offer the same incentives."

I say, "Right, true. But still, if we somehow managed restoration of the wetlands and a new, all-better levee system, and if there were confidence in that, and complete faith in the protection of it, well, then, maybe F.D.R. would return and be our president."

"There exists a morale problem," Adam says, "Nonetheless. New Orleans has much in its favor. A major airport. It's a reasonable distance to either coast. They need to establish a police force and a legal system. Then, if the mains don't allow raw sewage into the water supply, this'll be a goddamn good place to film."

[141]

It's around sundown. The sky's pearl and pink. I'm in the dark of my parked car, stopped in what was once Storyville, watching people—a gang of kids with buzzed heads playing street hockey in the last light, smacking too hard and sending their pucks into the grounged out yards. Their parents in cutoffs, toting beer bottles, rising occasionally to shout at the kids or chase after them for a couple feet.

There's a grill smell that's a little larger than the lumber smell over the neighborhood at this hour. Hammers and saws and sanders still going. This seems like a small town. One in a cluster of different small towns.

The sky over the street holds a single star and a moon white as milk. In the center of the road, a tall transvestite, hair bundled high in a towel, lurches this way, now that.

[142]

Petal's gazing at me. She says, "Want me to go around and start slapping people?"

"No, I'm O.K.," I say. "Speak softly, though. You don't want to get in trouble."

"Oh, like what? They'd turn a water hose on me?"

"Perhaps. Or put you in solitary confinement."

"Umm. I already have a private room," Petal says.

I say, "I bet they have a different kind of private room. Different altogether, thematically. A room way down in their basement."

"There're no basements, baby. You're in the South."

"Well, I don't know then," I say. "But something. They could give you worse drugs!"

"No," she says, "they couldn't."

[143]

- No more phone calling the archbishop in the wee hours.

- No more going out dressed in leaves.

- I'm through popping out of the car trunk at revival meetings.

- I'm mostly done with cutting the nipples out of bras.

- Never again wearing the Trotsky t-shirt or a newspaper sailor hat to church.

[144]

You had better get to the point with Adam. Better wrap things up, because that's what he's doing. In a blink, he'll be done and have nothing more for you. Even though you're still there in his room, or his car, his office, his bed. What are you supposed to? You go *where* next?

[145]

I'm preparing to go into the Atchafalaya Prescription Center and pick up Adam's meds; happy to sit here as long as it takes to get prepared.

In the car next to mine, a baby's turned around in its safety chair, watching its mother under the hatchback as she loads groceries and organizes sacks.

I have just backed my motorized seat over my reading glasses.

But, unfair to blame the baby. I can get another pair. There's probably an optician still practicing in one of the neighboring states.

[146]

The father is scooping snow peas onto his plate. Here, at the dining table with his wife beside him and me opposite.

The mother's silver hair is in a perfect chignon, or so she assured me, whatever a chignon could be, and whatever it's worth, her assurance.

Now the smells of basil and pepper jelly as wild mushrooms and roast chicken are presented.

The father's barely eating. It's as if I'm keeping him from going home for the day. He stops using his silverware, and looks up at me. He says nothing, goes back to his dinner. He pauses, puts his knife and fork down, looks up at me again.

A man dressed in chef's whites and a popup hat peeks in on us, but no one talks to him either. We all finish eating finally and no one talks.

Now the father drops a lump of sugar into his coffee and stirs it delicately. "I'd like to know where my sons are," he says.

"Adam is up watching horseracing TV," I tell him.

"And Saunders?" asks the father. He pats his mouth with his napkin.

"I can't say."

"You can't say?"

"No."

"But you understand why I'm asking you," he says.

"Yes," I say, "all the reasons. All understood thoroughly."

[147]

Saunders is at my place dropping off Collie, and struggling as hard as I've seen or heard anyone to enunciate and sit in a chair.

Collie's bustling around, serving me and her dad glasses of ice water. Saunders sips his, exaggerates a frown, tosses the water on her.

"That's it, that's it," I say, yanking her away from him.

Her blouse is soaked at the collar. She looks puzzled, like she's wondering where she left something, maybe in another room.

"Oh, come on, people, take a joke," Saunders says.

Now he's snatched up my water glass. He's clowning around, sloshing and splashing on himself. "A joke," he says again.

[148]

I'm warning Lucien his life is going to be lived in the van. "Ten weeks of pre-production. Twenty hours each week. Four hours per day."

"That's backwards," he says. "You count them the other way, where you *start* with the hours per day, then ascend."

This gets a sigh out of me. Now, a couple beats of silence.

"Let me finish with what I prepared to teach you today. Then we'll both take a moment to find it interesting that you have an *opinion* about how to count out the hours one will fucking spend in the van."

"Okie doke," says Lucien.

I say, "For ten weeks! Starting when you find a location. Which you'll come back to, getting things straight. Twenty goddamn hours a week, you'll put in! Because you will return to the spot with the art director, and the cinematographer, then the storyboard fucking artist, on and on. And each and every motherfucking visit will cost you four or more hours."

He says, "Maybe this isn't *all* about me."

[149]

Through the windows is the sound of wind in the freakish, fantastic trees. The parents' boxer dog is tearing in and out of the room, bounding incompetently at the windowsills.

Saunders sits on the floor over an opened newspaper. With a ball-peen hammer, he's smashing his electronic pager to plastic dust. I don't know why he's spending his energies this way.

"I'm an alcoholic," he says.

I accept this from him with a nod, but say, "Doesn't mean you always have to act like one."

I say, "Let's take a different turn and play chess or something."

"I'm fine with that," he says. He rises off the floor and goes around the room in search of his set. "Didn't know you liked to play."

"Well, I don't like to, when I'm not in the mood."

"Uh-huh," says he, positioning the game board and its pieces.

I say, "And, how the hell hard could it be?"

[150]

I'm at a table, waiting for my food order, and can't remember what it is, and I don't care. Some food or other. There's one server for all these two hundred people.

The woman on my left is telling me something. She says, "There's no ER staffs. My neighbor fell and then had her spleen operated on? But that wasn't bad enough. The hospital didn't have a anesthesiologist. 'Cause I guess there's none left. So, you know what they did? Borrowed one, and got it to come down here from Keesler Air Force Base. Bet that cost a ton. 'Cause it's in Biloxi, Mississippi. Which is in a different state."

[151]

"I won't be able to work tomorrow," says Lucien.

"Oh, sure, O.K.," I say. "Taking the day off?"

"It won't be just the *one* day, is the thing."

"Well, that's fine," I say. "But, you seem all right. Does this have to do with your grandma?"

"No," he says. "No."

"The fucking hell, Lucien."

"It's like a nightmare," he says. "I'm in a government-issued trailer. My dogs are whining, *they're* hungry. I'm trying to keep out of going to jail. Now I got the worst part of it starting up tomorrow."

"Starting up tomorrow, when . . ."

He lowers his head, and carefully sets down his coffee cup, which, although he's been sipping from it for twenty minutes, is still three-quarters full.

I say, "Please, God, don't permit this to go on any longer. It isn't right, and it isn't fair. Don't allow him to keep making me guess."

He looks acutely embarrassed. "Tomorrow's the beginning of house arrest that I gotta serve a sentence of, for ten days. Tomorrow'll count as Day Number One, just as soon as they come and put the, you know, thing locked onto my ankle."

"And why?"

He says, "I was in fact, shoplifting. Then what happened next was, I did get caught." He picks up his coffee cup again and stares into it miserably.

"Your grandmother?"

"Unbeknownst to her," Lucien says.

"What happens when she does find out?"

"She'll, first off, explode," he says. "Then maybe throw me down the well."

[152]

This isn't as pretty as I planned to look to go see my husband. There's just no time to make the big improvements that looking pretty would entail:

- fat camp.
- the swimsuit I wore at seventeen.
- Bach Suite Number 3 in D major played on the cello by Yo-Yo Ma.
- a walk through the carwash.
- my grandfather, back from the dead.
- a motorcycle.

chapter 7

[153]

I CALL IN THE morning to check on Lucien, and his grandmother answers the phone. "He's indisposed," she says.

"Well, I wanted to hear how things went with him, is all. Make sure everything's O.K."

"Indisposed," she tells me. "Like I said."

[154]

"Discussing water," Adam says, and pats the place beside him on the loveseat for me to sit.

He says, "Yeah, statistically, that is the case. For days and weeks after a hurricane, skies are very clear."

"And that's not just a superstition. Not a coincidence," says Saunders.

"Is that like a question, bro? No. It's neither of those." Adam is holding a fountain pen over some papers. He smiles, absently scribbling some lightning lines.

"So, there's no chance of collecting rainwater," I say, and they cast their glances at me.

I say, "Just here to empty the ashtrays. It'll take me two minutes and then I'll be out of your hair."

Saunders reaches and gives my knee a squeeze. I notice both Bait & Switch are wearing pressed shirts today and at their wrists, beaming silver cufflinks.

"You know, the Navy has a device—" he begins.

"Sure," Adam says. "They used it in Biloxi. Mobile desalination units. Which convert seawater to purer than EPA. It's done with a Reverse Osmosis membrane. You know who cooked that one up? Dow."

"Hmm," Saunders says. "Winner of the Company with the Most Horrific Karma Award."

"This is called the Morning Room, this room?" I ask.

"Maybe it was originally," says Saunders.

Adam says, "It's still the Morning Room. Conceived as a ladies' parlor for entertaining neighbor ladies each morning. For the dispersal of information and news."

I say, "Now you're both looking at me and waiting for a punch line from me, about how nowadays we have CNN or email. Well, you can both just wait."

"She's not our little toy," Saunders says with a shake of the head.

[155]

"You're dreaming," the mother says. "It just doesn't have the ring of truth. I can't believe you're seriously going along with all this. Are you for real?"

She says, "You're thinking *exactly* what they want you to think. You've swallowed the bait, whole. Swallowed it hook, line, and sinker."

[156]

I go by Lucien's FEMA trailer, to check up on him and see how he's doing, and to show him some photographs I took in Storyville the other day.

"No way," his grandmother says at the door.

"I'm—"

"Elsewhere," she says. "You are elsewhere. Go bother somebody else."

It's theoretically possible this person is his grandmother. She's maybe as old as thirty-four or thirty-five. Mathematically, possible, but I don't want to develop any wider understanding of a situation in which a Cracker Barrel hostess with gum and scarlet lipstick and a Cleopatra haircut and wearing socks with her size-five Capezio shoes is Lucien's grandmother. That there's plenty for me to know.

And that she's mean. That there's a meanness she's been dipped into many, many times. Coats of meanness she then allowed to harden.

[157]

In a City That Is Only Seven Miles Long

- In '06, New Orleans far surpassed every other city in America for being the bloodiest. In '07, New Orleans surpassed itself.

- For '06 there was 1 murder conviction.

- Less than 12 percent of those charged with murder have gone to prison at all.

- 85 percent of New Orleans' residents say that "people being killed" is a primary concern.

- There are altogether about 1400 police officers on duty in New Orleans at present. Over half of them are new.

- A CNN-authenticated autopsy shows that an unarmed, retarded man with no criminal record was shot in the back and killed by police.

- More than 50 former NOPD officers are in prison, 2 on death row.

- Add to that 8 former officers, who have now been indicted for murder and attempted murder.

[158]

I've come to pick up Collie and caught the glint of her buzzed red head out back here in the yard. She's deep in, standing under a ruined magnolia tree, peering up into its branches. There are fallen dysfunctional blossoms, looking like killed pelicans, all around.

"What's going on?" I ask, closer in.

She keeps her eyes on the branches. "Scooter's stuck! Way high in the tree."

I say, "No, you can't have a cat named Scooter."

"It's from before that time it was on the news."

"You know, you can successfully change a cat's name. Is this the yellow one that's so cute? How about Butterscotch or Honey Boy? Honey Boy! Wouldn't that be better? We could all start calling him it right away."

"No, you stupid! It's a woman!" says Collie.

Crying.

I say, "That's all right, it's O.K. I know just what to do."

She looks at me.

"And it's not call the Fire Department. They don't care and it would take them days to get here. No, no. You call a tree surgeon. Those're the people who trim and chop up trees. They have all the good equipment."

"What if they moved away?" she asks.

"That's a possibility, I admit. But still not to worry. I know people with cranes."

[159]

Late night, at Café du Monde:

A voice says, "We lost all the cooks in the back of the house, immediately. Lost most of our servers, who can't ever come back.

Where the people in the food industry lived, those are who took the worst flooding."

A toddler who shouldn't be awake points at me with a baton.

The fellow beside me shuts his attaché and locks it with a tiny key.

Another voice joins in, saying, "These people lost it all. They can't afford to rebuild. What's gone is gone, and they gone."

They serve me a straw and my milk in a little waxed carton.

A crazy man leans across his seat and leers my way as if he's greeting a streetwalker.

The same voice as before says, "Walk up and down this very street if you don't believe me. Take a good look at all the Now Hiring signs in each and every window. What else do you think those could mean?"

[160]

I've dropped by to see Lucien and drawn the grandmother immediately to the door, now glaring at me.

I rattle a paper document in front of her face, and say, "This! Is! Business! Very, very important to him. This! Is! His! Work!"

She opens the door a teensy crack.

I say, "There are fifteen different things to consider here. I need to talk to him, and I need that talk now."

"Listen, you," she says. "Whoever the hell you are."

In the background, her TV cries: "Tons of games in high depth!"

She says, "Don't think you can come banging on my door whenever you feel like it, making demands. Do you hear me? Do you think you can just barge on in here and order me around? Who the hell are you?"

"A friend, O.K.?"

"That's what you think? That you're somebody's friend and therefore you're entitled to waltz into my place and start passing out orders."

"She wasn't running away!" says the TV.

"Maybe I'm busy right now," says the grandmother. "Maybe I'm right in the middle of something, and don't want to deal with you bamming on my door anytime you see fit."

"I came to speak to Lucien," I say. "Whom you know as Paul. I came in good faith. Now quit insulting me."

"Insulting you? You're on *my* property, sister."

"Well, kind of," I say.

"That does it," she says, pushing the door on me.

"Wait, wait . . ."

"For what? Now you're gonna apologize?"

"I *do* want to apologize."

"Too late," she says, putting weight on the door.

I say, as she's closing me all the way off, "I am so truly sorry, cunt."

[161]

I'm stumbling into the messed-up street, babbling things I didn't get a chance to say.

"Where're you going?" Lucien croaks, and his face appears at a screened window of the trailer.

"Away," I say. "At your grandmother's recommendation."

"You don't have to run off," he says, sounding young, and sounding little.

I'm approaching the window. "Yeah. Listen, I really alienated her, is the thing. So we're not going to be able to be friends now. Or ever, she and I, probably. It's too bad, and do let her know sometime that I'm sorry for being disrespectful. Sincerely am."

He's looking at me from behind the screen.

"Just tell her that I felt really bad," I say.

"Why don't you wait until she's gone," says Lucien. "She has to be at work in a few minutes."

"What does she do, you don't mind my asking."

"Aw, she's, you know, an escort. But it's money we direfully need. I don't see that much wrong with it."

"Hell no. Good for her," I say. "And man, has she kept herself together. You two look practically the same age."

"Oh," he says from behind the screen, and grins, "no, no. 'Grandmother' is something she just puts down on forms."

"Oh, boy."

He says, "Now, wait 'til you hear the rest of it. There's more to it than what you could imagine. See, *this* is why we keep it a secret from people!"

"And there may have been great wisdom in your decision to do that," I say.

"She took full care of me," he says, "all right? Out of the goodness and kindness of her own free will. She could've, just as easily, dumped me off onto strangers. Who then might've turned around and revealed a worse side to themselves. You can't tell! Not until after the damage is done. But she didn't choose that easier path. No, ma'am. Instead, she chose to take me in with her. Without one second's thought. Which I appreciate, gratefully. And she always, always treated me just like a grandmother."

"There's a twist," I say.

[162]

Lucien's outside the bathroom door, shouting at me: "Don't you think you should come *out* of there by now? My grandma's only working for the lunch hour. She's liable to be back home here at any minute."

I say, "Not until I've made sure there's nothing any good in her medicine cabinet."

"Oh, me," Lucien says. "Then you ought to know there exists a half bath. It's off of her bedroom. So, I guess you need to go there next and loot."

[163]

I say to Collie, thumping my forefinger on the table for emphasis, "Because water . . . makes . . . electricity . . . mad."

[164]

There was one other husband, for a time in the early '90s—Kenny. Who got up from our dining table one evening after he finished his meal, ambled downstairs to the street, and jumped in front of a moving car.

Then he wouldn't speak about it, not to me. I assume he talked with his doctors at the hospital, as they kept him for months, and loaded him up with different bottles of medication on his release. I just wasn't very intelligent. He took the meds until they ran out, then didn't feel he needed refills. And there wasn't anything theatrical to indicate he was still messed up. I thought there'd at least be bouts of weeping. No, only this flattened version of Kenny. He had really become so bland. I was the most surprised of anyone when he slid into the restroom at a cocktail party and slashed up both his wrists. But the ambulance came in time. They wouldn't nowadays. We just didn't last long after that, he and I.

[165]

- A Double Shoulder Holster will hold two medium-sized pistols. This type of carry is a good alternative to packing one gun that is very powerful but simply too large for your body type.

- Bandolier Holsters are a must for heavy guns and scoped handguns. These holsters are worn at chest center, over the solar plexus. They have an adjustable harness and are completely comfortable once in place.

- Bra Holsters are inexpensive, cloth holsters made of soft, washable materials that protect your gun and your skin. Note that these holsters are drawn along with the gun and need not be removed, as your gun will fire through them just as easily.

- Hip Holsters can be worn comfortably in front or in back of the hipbone. If you're carrying a wide-bodied auto-matic, such as a Glock or a Sigma, position the holster right over a trouser-loop to redistribute the weight and to prevent sagging. Take extra care that this holster doesn't jab your upper thigh when you sit down.

[166]

"Well, what about this place?" I ask Petal. "Now that you've been here a bit. Anything good you can say?"

"Thinking," she says, narrowing her eyes, and tilting her head back on her shoulders.

"Do whatever you need."

"The meals are right on time," she says.

"Oh, yeah? Good, good. That would be a definite plus."

"She says, "And, I have to acknowledge, that with the existing setup, it is very easy to meet people."

"Is that right? Well, and I'm sure you have done. Anything else? Other advantages to being here?"

She says, "The doctors never get personal with you, or inquire into anything personal. They're careful about that."

"No? Huh. I would think, the opposite actually. That they would dig deep down into your life. For diagnosis. Treatment. Also, to help them decide which specific therapy would be the most effective for you."

"They keep to the charts," Petal says. "They only question you to verify information."

"Oh, O.K. Well, I can understand that approach. That's prudent of them. So you don't start feeling cornered. Right, right. They don't want to add to your stress load. They get what's necessary, get down all the pertinent information, and confirm your—"

"Name," she says. "That your name is the same one they have in the charts."

"Ah," I say, nodding.

"Their whole thing's consistency," she says.

"At the same time, they're confirming that you know you *are* yourself," I say.

[167]

From the United Methodist Church:

• "Use as an outline a sermon based on lectionary readings for the day.

• Personalize the story.

• Open with a short anecdote about Hurricane Katrina, either yours or a story you wish to share.

• Speak of seeing Jesus in the face of the survivors.

• Express gratitude."

[168]

Adam has a box of photographs opened on his lap. He's thumbing through them as we sit.

"Here's one of Hazel," he says, passing me a shot of his first wife.

I'm studying the Polaroid.

"It's a flattering picture," he says. "One of the best she ever had taken."

"No, I remember what she looked like," I say.

We knew each other years ago, from a Far Eastern Art class we both took at Tulane. She sat near me. Tall, blonde, in flower-print skirts all the time, kind of busty, in white cotton tank tops. I remember she moved like a giraffe, and stood canted to the side like a giraffe does. I sometimes hold that recollection in mind beside an image of a younger Adam. And then, there they are, as they were, a lovely married couple.

Hazel always wanted to move to New England and live in Maine, is why the two divorced, Adam told me. He told me that and I had to admire him for doing so. Nothing but contentment until one day they fought about Maine.

[169]

Lucien has a pocket road atlas clenched in his left hand and with his right index finger he's tracing a route. He says to me, "You have familiarity with the Louisiana plantations, isn't that correct? Enough where you could attest that you *scouted* them all at one time and know everything about them?"

"Altogether wrong," I say. "Sorry. They're out of my jurisdiction."

He says, "But supposing I wanted photographs of them? For a formal Location Scout portfolio that I want to build up. You could help fill me in on the minute details, couldn't you not?"

"Well no, not really. None of the details. I could direct you to several, but so could a tourist map. There're only two I've even been inside, in St Francisville, and those were most-cursory visits."

"Cursory," Lucien says.

"Really quick. I don't like them. They creep me out. And depress me. They've got maybe some ballrooms and nice spiral staircases for you to admire. Big fucking whoop."

"Didn't mean to upset your feelings," Lucien says as he puts his atlas away.

"I'm obnoxious," I say.

He asks, "What about where Audubon stayed and studied? Couldn't that one single *one* be all right with you?"

"Oakley," I say. "But it doesn't look all that great."

Over there, a crowd of men are getting seated, all talking hard and at once.

Lucien looks at me across the table. It's possible he's reluctant to speak.

Out the windows, the sky is a brilliant orange.

I raise my empty wineglass and clink it against his. We are, after all, here to acknowledge the end of his house arrest.

He lifts off the jacket of his charcoal suit. He's got on black suspenders and a pristine dress shirt that's unbuttoned at the collar.

We both sit back; both gaze blankly at the table's centerpiece—a giant magnolia blossom with waxy, dark leaves.

"I wonder if that's fake," I say. "Since the salinity of the flood water annihilated magnolia trees."

"I've been thinking about chef school," says Lucien.

"Oh no, please don't," I say.

"Why should I not? What's wrong with it?"

"Nothing. Or, there's probably nothing very wrong with it. Just, don't want you going off the air right now."

[170]

I'm walking on Toulouse.

Past a fellow on a stoop reading a detective novel with a lurid cover.

Past a clean-swept cobblestone courtyard that's shaded by sweet olive trees.

Past a drunk man lurching backward a step, forward a step, backward a step.

Past a woman slathering the fretwork on her windows with turquoise paint.

Past a disturbed teenager in makeup and jewelry who's crouched, clawing at the air, snarling at the passersby.

[171]

Saunders and I are climbing around in bed, high as kites, going over each other slowly, attentively, as if the important thing at this hour is to learn every last detail. As if the only thing.

Being with him, whenever I'm not, doesn't exist. I'm not allowed to think about it. Would not dare.

[172]

"So, what *do* you do all day?" Adam asks me.

"Locations, still the job," I say. "I go out, occasionally drop by the office. Check in with some people. Sit down, start maybe looking at different things. Drink coffee. Try to decide where-to next, and what next." I shrug. "Same job as everybody has, in a way."

He says, "Suppose you were scouting this place."

"No."

"Why not?" he asks, smiling. "I think it's nice."

"Of course it is. But, there are a whole lot of reasons. Many, many, many."

"Give me a such as."

"The pond," I say. "The willows, the ironwork, statue, swans, so on and so forth. You've got a fence on one side, that's been there and has to stay there. Really dense woods on two other sides. Mammoth trees, with branches that're ridiculous. A path that can barely accommodate even a person."

"You couldn't—"

"Build like a rail system that winds its way through? No. Then, the pond itself. You step one foot in, the water goes to chowder. So you drain it, fine, take out all the fish and lily fronds or whatever, rocks, algae. Clear the floor, and drain every drop of water, lay down a whole new liner, install a much better pump, put in new water . . ."

"Got it," he says.

"Not in here either. Those windows? Too high, and, I've measured them, they're only twenty-eight inches. So, the last choice is bring in every piece of equipment through the door. We've got doorway dollies. But at this point, the charm's kind of gone out of the room, and the wallpaper's going to get ruined. Believe me on this, I've disqualified every room in the house using much the same criterion."

He says, "I never understood why the background's so important anyway."

"Well, it's film," I say. "If it doesn't involve special effects, or isn't a musical, or action with cattle stampeding, but just shows conversations and walking around and the like, there must be something to entertain the eyes.

[173]

I'm cruising a little ways out tonight, traveling upriver. The sky is a grape color, fixed with a cartoon quarter of moon.

There are lighted oil barges, and grain barges on the Mississippi, behemoth freighters bound for sea.

Nearer dawn I see tree-lined avenues, fields of indigo, King cotton, cane, cows, high-tension lines, cricket oil wells, now stretches of winding country roads, moss-covered monuments, oddly still bayous, long alleys of arching Live Oak trees.

[174]

Listening to old music. Smoking some boo that was sold to me by a Cajun waitress at The Camellia Cafe. Getting reefer requires some effort. I have to try and even pay for it on occasion. In New Orleans, nothing would prevent me from purchasing liquor ever.

- Not if I were a naked baby.
- On hands and knees.
- Crawling down the goddamn center of the street.
- At four in the morning.
- On Easter Sunday.

[175]

"Now there're no permits or fees for filming in Louisiana, unless you're talking about filming on state property, but even those kinds of fees are usually waived," I say to Lucien. "The City of New Orleans either. No fees, no permits. Charges and permissions, yes, if you want to use city services, and those include—you need to write all these down—cemeteries, explosions, the Historic Quarter, parking, blocking off streets, NOPD, Transit Authority, sanitation, and for the removal of streetlights or other city fixtures."

"You mean, I will have to go to the people in authority and *get* these permissions. As in, have to obtain them somehow. You and I. We, us, will have to."

"Well, no," I say. "We work for a production agency for crap's sake. It's all right if we leave for them a few things to do."

"Aren't they gonna mind?"

I let out a sigh. "What do you mean, Lucien? Do you mean, mind because it's really our job? No. It's not our job," I say, shaking my head. "So, what you're wondering is why you had to hear about it then. Am I right?"

"If that's not going to make you mad. Or mad-der," he says ducking his shoulders a little.

I clap my hand on his back. "Not mad," I say, "in the slightest. But this is why. Because permit stuff varies a lot from state to state. Sometimes, therefore, you have to pass information, such as this, along to out-of-towners. That way, see, they don't have to guess."

[176]

I don't know but it feels late. Ever since Katrina I haven't *needed* my watch. An hour ago, maybe, someone from the kitchen brought us a silver tray with nut muffins and hashed pears, tea in china cups.

Here's Adam, peering blandly at his laptop screen.

"What're you up to?" I ask him.

"Nothing. Or, you know. Nothing," he says.

"I've been reading about a gunboat officer," I say, balancing the loosened script on my knees and letting many pages of it drop to the floorboards.

This is Adam's bedroom. Hand-screened wallpaper. A little row of three lime trees in Rocaille planters. A canopied bed.

I look at all that, and at the tray of food we ignored, through a frame I'm pretending with my fingers.

"Please, stop it," says Adam.

"Why? I was just—"

He says, "Baby, I'm hideously sick."

chapter 8

[177]

Building & Industry

- Looters are stealing new appliances as soon as returning residents have them installed.

- The shortage of plumbers is severe.

- Under Louisiana's codes, plumbers from outside states are not permitted to work. Contractors hurried legislation against making any post-Katrina exception to this rule.

- Undocumented Workers, hired at the most meager wage, make up a quarter of the reconstruction force.

- Because Undocumented Workers carry away whatever cash they have earned, they are often robbed of it.

- 259 government contracts meant for small businesses actually went to big (ineligible) companies.
- The largest part of the workforce consists of prison laborers.

[178]

We're sitting outside at the Laurel Bakery. Lucien's beside me, sipping a latte, listening to me advise this guy.

I'm saying, "There are endless amounts of swampland along the Mississippi, and along the little rivers that connect to it—Pearl River, the Red River, Atchafalaya. Perfect for shooting, 'cause there's nobody there. On the north shore of the lake you've got marshes and bayous—Cocodrie, Bayou Teche, Cue De Tortue.

"And you don't have to worry. It's not that bad. The whole trick is, you need a good road for the trucks and equipment. Then if you're near hotels and restaurants and not too far from the airport. But the local crew know the swamps, and they have plenty of contacts who are guides and boat operators. All we have to do is, first, get a good road."

"Don't ever let me do that again, gobble on like a turkey," I say to Lucien when the producer is gone. "Throw your beverages on me, if need be. Anything you can think of to bring about my silence."

"I will not," he says.

"Because why?"

"First," he says, "I'm not that type of person. Second, you're kind of a bad ass. Third, who can say how that guy is gonna react? Fourth, which should have been first, we need the business."

"I absolutely know he's not signing on," I say.

"Is that for a fact?"

"Fact."

"Well, then I'm sorry I sat here the whole time, and that I bothered to wear these good pants."

"Those are good pants. After my husband saw you, he said to ask who's your tailor."

"I don't have a tailor."

"It was praise," I say. "Now, hear me on the other. This producer's only down here to advertise himself. He's not serious. Don't know how I know that with any certainty but I do."

Near us, a freckled woman jumps up from her table and hugs a busty friend.

Lucien says, "I'm just getting started with clothes, I do realize that. I'm also trying desperately to keep things protected from mould."

"Wrap everything in bags that breathe. Like canvas. Not plastic," I say.

"Really? Where did you get that? From your husband? His suit today had like the high armholes. That means a big price tag. I noticed that and the wide shoulders. Slightly wide."

"Bought off the peg," I say.

There's a man jogging through our tables to catch the streetcar, kicking up some of the crepe myrtle that has fallen all over the sidewalk.

"I shouldn't judge all producers by this one example," says Lucien.

I say, "Plenty of others who are just as bad or worse."

Here are two workmen, one slapping the other's shoulder as they lower side-by-side into their seats.

Now a clergyman bustles by in a tremendous hurry.

"I dreamed nobody knew what day it was," I say.

"That might not be so bad," says Lucien. "Might've just been telling you it was no specific day."

[180]

I have memories of being in love with Adam, sure. Of the music we were listening to before its sound became a ting in a bucket.

[181]

"You document everything, right? We have forms you fill in with the information they need. The existing lights. Any immovable objects. The closest hospital. So on, and so on. You also have to draw little diagrams to show the layout of the grounds. Or to indicate there's a narrow bridge or a steep grade. And for the production van to take this alternate route. Which you will have figured out," I say.

"How will I have?" asks Lucien.

"With the brains, in your head."

"Ma'am, I don't know what a production van even *is*."

"It's just a truck with a generator on the rear of its tractor thing, usually. We only need to know what we need to know, Lucien. It's sixty feet long. It weighs ten tons. Not whose favorite truck it is. That's not our business."

"You don't have to bark at me," says he.

"Sorry. My husband's sick, and I'm just afraid you're going to get stuck."

I say, "Use my van, if anything like that happens. But keep it immaculately clean for driving these people around. Remember to carry I.D."

[182]

There's a surgeon here in the waiting room talking to the twins' father, nodding, talking some more, hands in his coat's big patch pockets.

Adam is not the one getting a new liver today, it turns out.

Saunders is a few seats down from me. He has his eyes fully closed and I'm not certain he's awake.

What a world. Up there in the corner is a giant TV. The sound is muted but the screen shows a couple of wrestlers, against a cherry-red backdrop, turning in their strange embrace.

[183]

"Good, I get to leave," says Adam.

"I don't like this," I say.

"Which this? My leaving?"

I say, "No, oddly, that part's O.K. All the rest of it, I hate. That hamster, Doctor Gainslings. The dinginess. Tiny, dirty, Old West–looking rooms. These blue curtains. Nothing is clean! And they're all high school kids. From the fifties. The religious factor, which'd be great if it weren't the hootenanny, smiley-face, balloon-give-out kind, just like these depressing fucking posters they've got up. That should say, 'Have a Bright and Sunny Death'."

"It's entirely O.K. with me if you're having a psychotic break-down," says Adam.

"I'm so horribly, horribly sorry," I say.

The father appears in the doorway. His face shows he's been listening, lurking closeby. "They know what they're doing here. You can be sure of that much," he says. He props his hands on his buttocks, walks around to the opposite side of Adam's bed.

"Just ignore me," I say. "It's a quirk in my nature. I come from a dissatisfied family."

"You do not," Adam says.

The father says, "Then there's something wrong with your family, and you should question them about it."

"I have," I say. "But they still haven't given me a satisfactory explanation."

"She's right to be a little circumspect," says Adam.

"No, my view," the father says, "is circumspect. Your wife's is confrontational."

I say, "I have the normal number of ears."

The father shifts forward a little. "I'm the one she's confronting. She does so by opposing my decisions at every turn, and by being a busybody."

"Ooh," Adam says, cringing. "You should call her a twat or something, Father. It'd be less offensive."

"Quite a lot less," I say.

[184]

"This has to do with the daughter," says Petal, after I've repeated the father's words. "Especially that stuff about questioning his judgment."

"What? Tell me," I say.

"Ah, it's this whole thing. Julia had an online romance, that they, the parents, shut down. Guarding their money. After she'd told them she was engaged. She fought and fought about it, up until the day she died. I guess it must have been confusing. Usually, they indulged her every whim. She was mentally handicapped, remember."

I shake my head, no.

"She wanted to have a wedding," Petal says.

"Well, did they check the guy out?" I ask. "Maybe he was serious, and mentally retarded as well."

"That wouldn't have won them over too much," Petal says. "Can we call the screws now and get me out of here?"

[185]

"Why this picture?" I ask Lucien, waving a snapshot he took of some gargantuan bumblebees that are somebody's lawn ornaments.

He shrugs, a little embarrassed.

"No, I want this," I say. "If you'll sell it to me. It really needs to hang in a prominent place where it can break my heart all the time."

[186]

"We can't just take a spin through the area," I tell the producer. Kip Kaiser is his unconvincing name.

"I'm a filmmaker," he says, with his hands pressed over his heart. "This is my proverbial thing."

I raise my brows and close my eyelids in response.

"You're worried about the tough guys," he says. "Don't. You'll see, my love. They'll all but bend over backwards. Because, here's a surprise for you. They tend to view me as an ally. If that makes any sense."

I won't say it does. It doesn't.

He says, "They see me like Misters Pitt, Connick Junior, Marsalis, Demme, Spike Lee . . ."

I say, "I'm in hell."

"They see me as someone with the power and means to get the word out. Who knows? Maybe do some good."

"There's still! A huge! Amount of debris!" I say.

"Oh, and that's so shocking," he says, giving a series of sarcastic nods. "Darlin', you don't know so much about filmmakers. Shocking is our bread and butter."

He puts a hand out in my honor, saying, "You're being careful with me. That, I appreciate."

I say, "I wasn't. I wouldn't. I'm not. This is like a traffic report! There's still debris all over the streets, O.K.? Down there in the Chertoff Sewage Puddle and Michael J. Brown Latrine. Now I'm exhausted! Whole fucking houses were thrown into the fucking streets and there's still debris."

He smiles, seats himself on the edge of a table. "So, that's what you're hyperventilating about," he says. "So, there it is. All right. Easy enough. I'll hire a work crew to clear a way through. Probably cost less than you'd think."

"We're not going," I say promptly.

"Oh, don't get fucking nutsoid on me," he says, and slides down from his seat on the table. Approaching, as if to gather me in his arms.

"No, I'm not taking you there," I say. "As far as I'm concerned, you don't get to go."

[187]

Here's a family of three, in a Thai restaurant near my place. The parents sit across from each other at a round table with a red table-cloth. They're nibbling chicken wings. Their son is on all fours, eating from a dish on the tiled floor. I'm just supposed to watch. The mother doesn't raise her head ever. The father keeps on eating and keeps on gripping the back of the boy's neck.

"You don't wanna have to go out to my truck," he says in a loud-enough voice.

The servers, the hostess, the cook, the owners have all rushed into the room, rushed out, rushed back in. The other diners have got up and left and come back.

"Don't interfere" the father says to anyone. And says, "This is the disciplining of my child." Like a sign over the tire shop of his behavior.

The only things I can think of to do meanwhile aren't any use to anybody.

Drink all the club soda in my glass in one breath.

Open my coin purse and count through the change.

Check for ladyhead dimes or wreath pennies.

Ask the server how club soda is made.

Put silver coins in a single stack, copper coins in another.

[188]

"The great thing about Shreveport," says Lucien, and I sigh, but motion for him to go on, fine, I'm listening.

"This guy I know named Cooley? He moved there after Katrina and he's already advanced his way up to Film Loader. He's very, very nearly in the union, in fact. But what he told me? Is that with the same identical skills, if he were in Hollywood, he would starve to death.

"I have no trouble believing that."

"I'm saying *that's* how fast it's booming in Shreveport right now. All on account of film."

I say, "That grates."

"Why don't you, instead of building up a steam of resentment," says Lucien, "*profit* by it and relocate?"

"No," I say. "I couldn't do that. The thing that makes you any good as a location scout is knowing streets and neighborhoods, and what could go with what. I don't have the fucking first clue about Shreveport."

"You could go there," he says. "You could learn it all."

"No. That's for somebody else."

"Who else is better to?"

"Shreveportians, I guess," I say. "Just not me."

[189]

Sex, at my place, in silence, and under a sheet.

Not silence. I can still hear muffled car honks and brakes and tires, the next door neighbor's cat, and laughter now from some huddle of men, a National Guard helicopter going over, the air fan, the plumbing's rumble, the bed when we move, a child somewhere having a dream, the high whine of the streetcar, the little voice of a neighbor's television, freighter horns on the Mississippi, now Saunders' long breathing against my chest as he's slipping off into sleep.

[190]

My phone sounds and calling me is Kip the producer, asking where he should live if he decides to move here.

"I'm about ninety-nine percent decided," he tells me.

"First, rent a car," I say, "and drive up and down Prytania. Check out all the cross streets between Saint Charles and Magazine. I wouldn't recommend anything north of that. Also, look seriously at the Arts and Warehouse District. My place is an up-and-down on Julia, there. It's just north of the Quarter, so plenty lively, all hours. On-street parking. If you feel like you'd have to live *in* the Quarter, however, stick to the lower part, east of the Cathedral, where they've got the noise level somewhat more under control."

I can tell he isn't noting any of this, or even listening, at least not to me. Nor does he plan to move here or film here ever. On that, I'd bet a body part. He's probably already got digs in Shreveport.

[191]

Lucien and I have been butlered into a parlor where Fear & Loathing are lounging. There's a little drift of cigar smoke overhead, vacant seats on the leather couches, an old movie whispering on the television.

In our awkwardness, the four of us are sitting together, all staring at the set as if it had something urgent to offer, and as if the something were threatening to go forever away.

So we sit and regard the screen.

Adam says to anyone: "Seventy-five bucks if you can name the actor playing the Chief Petty Officer."

"I think—" Lucien says.

"Who?" asks my husband.

"Only if you feel like answering," I say, reaching to thump Lucien on the shoulder.

"Thank God you're here," Saunders says to me.

"That it could be Scott Wilson," says Lucien.

"Correct," I say, conking the end table with the heel of my hand. I'm not certain if Scott Wilson's right but neither does anyone else in this overprivileged place.

Adam pats a pocket and raises his hand to show that he's coming up empty. He gestures at Saunders, who stands and dutifully extracts a wallet from the hip of his jeans.

Beyond us are louvered French doors and then a gallery of citrus trees in Terra-Bella planters.

Saunders passes Lucien a hundred dollar bill.

"Aw, I don't have any of the change for this," Lucien says. "Can't we just forget about it? You guys shouldn't have to waste your hard-earned money on me."

"Well," I say, "I have an opinion. Three opinions. Yes, they should. It might as well go to you. And, lastly, you should allow disgust in your voice when you say 'hard-earned.'"

[192]

"No more mailing my laundry to the IRS," I tell Petal. "No more faking with crutches at the airport."

"I would probably," she says, "decline another Mohawk haircut."

"Through hiding in the bushes from people," I say. "I don't have enough guilt to do that anymore."

She says, "I'm never again spitting in the palm of my hand. Never getting out of here."

"Don't be nuts," I say. "Wait. That was a stupid choice of words. All anyone really thinks is that you might have an anger problem."

She's had her eyes closed. She opens them sleepily, and closes them again, shaking her head. "Nothing to do with that, don't you know. Now it's just about money and paying to keep me locked up."

She looks so pretty. Her champagne hair, immaculate skin, a gargantuan sweater. Her hands tug the sweater's sleeves down her wrists against some inner chill. Everything about her is graceful, even in her sickness and despair.

[193]

"I did what you told me," says Kip the producer. "But something didn't smell right. You need to explain to me specifically what is safe."

"Nowhere's safe," I say. Everyplace here is terrifying. The tax base dropped, so did civilization. Streetlights, traffic lights, police and fire departments, emergency services."

He says, "I mean neighborhoods."

"It's not safe and dangerous neighborhoods so much as safe and dangerous streets," I say. "And then safe and dangerous *parts* of streets. Quite specific."

"I thought you said 'dangerous parts of speech,' is why I'm smiling," he says.

And he is. There across the table from me, smiling.

I say, "You're not . . . a serious enough person for me to be talking to right now."

"Excuse me?"

"All right, I didn't mean that. I'm sure you're very serious."

He looks back and forth, flabbergasted. "Lady! I'm about as serious as they're ever going to come."

"Well, good, then, I'll go on. Don't call me 'lady.' What you mustn't listen to are these people telling you that the crime's all happening in Gentilly, or the Seventh Ward."

"No?" he asks, with a tilt of the head.

"No," I say. "It's a very irresponsible piece of misinformation. The murder victim, Helen Hill, for example? A filmmaker like yourself. You've got Central City just down from Tulane. It's had plenty of fatalities. Tremé is connected to the Quarter. The Marigny's skirted by the Florida and Desire neighborhoods Also, crime is spreading out, of course."

"Of course?"

"Yes, because the wealthier people *have* stuff."

"Huh, he says, and shakes his head, amused.

"All right, that's not the single reason. But the discussion about the other reasons is playing on a different channel. Back to where you should and shouldn't go. There's no directory. You pay attention and you ask people. When you go out, you go out with a group. You leave nothing in the car, ever. You don't pump gas alone."

"Do I rattle you, Queenie?" he asks.

I say, "You sure are trying to, furiously hard."

"Take that as a yes."

"Yeah, you do have an effect on me," I say. "You make me restless, and impatient."

"And you are not, normally?"

"Never," I say. "Like right now. I just want to hand you something, and have you scan it or stamp it so I can get out of here."

[194]

"What are you always reading about?" Lucien asks.

"I just like to study for some reason," I say. He doesn't need to know I'm reading *Hep C for Dummies*. "Probably got the habit from my folks."

"They forced you to study?"

"No, nobody forced me."

I say, "My parents were professors who would have been crappy at anything else."

"You're still lucky, though," he says. "I never even knew mine."

"Where did you and your grandmother live? Before you got the FEMA trailer?" I ask.

"In her car, for the between interval. Then before that, in a house. Her house. Your typical shotgun shack. That place took a *lot* of damage."

"Bad?"

He says, "Actually the house next to ours fell on it."

He drops his spoon into his coffee and slowly stirs. "The television fails to show people about the *sounds*. Like the animals? But they all, in my neighborhood, tried saving as many at a time as they could. I'd testify to that on a Bible. Of course, this is the way I end up with seven dogs. That I do love. Because what the dogs wouldn't do? Is leave from the sides of their dead owners. No way in hell. You had animal loyalty."

He says, "What *else* the TV couldn't show was the water. Where your average person gets an image of huge smooth waves, like for surfer boards. That is wrong. One hundred degrees the opposite. The true picture is, you've got animals and people skittering for dear life. Then chasing right behind them is water full of bushes and trees and the other animals mixed into it, probably dead. *Not* crystal blue clear water either. It's ugly gray. A dark, deepest, dark-black gray."

[195]

Sunset. I'm idling in the parking lot for a strip of shops. They're mostly closed shops that will never reopen. There's a vitamin center with a customer or two, and a paint store that has a little crowd. A children's shoe store, a frame maker's place, a mattress center. The custom lampshade shop is closed as could be.

Some of the citizenry is in view. Here's a boy in powder-blue clothes, slumped on a bench, staring glue-sniff-like at the pavement.

From out front of the garden store, a Creole woman is making off with a bag of mulch.

Now coming along past me is a disturbed-looking couple of teenagers. They are waddling after a creaking, listing, empty cart.

Sisters and brothers!

I don't know for how many minutes I've been sitting out here watching, too jittery to turn the engine off and go into a store and buy things. Equally unable to drive the fuck away.

[196]

Producer Kip says, "I don't understand why you blame so much on the Army Corps of Engineers."

"They're to blame," I say. "They built crappy levees in mushy soil, levees that sag five feet because they measured sea-level wrong. They're engineers! Those levees caused eighty percent of the flooding."

"You can't have it both ways," he says. "Only yesterday, you said the levees aren't protection anyway."

"And I was right about that," I say. "It's the cypress trees and wetlands that absorb the hit and make a storm less deadly. But The Army Corps ruined all that for us, too."

"Now you're just being ridiculous."

I say, "It *is* like I'm being ridiculous. They clawed up the marsh-land for canals and pipelines. That boosted the surge and made the storm ten times stronger. Add on to that, in their dicking around, they let in *saltwater*."

"What does that do?"

"Melts the marshland," I say, but wearily. I've had enough. There's no reason to convince this person.

We're stopped in the drive of his hotel. He's crouched inside the passenger door, doing a most-careful tally of his belongings that he's collected from off the seat and the dashboard and the floor of my vehicle.

These are the longest minutes! And for all of them I've had my hand in the air, holding out his leather sunglasses case for him. "How about we step it up," I say. "Long, long line behind you."

[197]

The Big Easy

• Rent increase in parishes with the worst storm
damage—200 percent.

• Number 1 reason for not returning—can't afford
the move.

• Damaged and destroyed firehouses—300.

• Firehouses repaired—0.

• Years before coastal communities are swallowed—10.

• Percentage of population living in coastal communities—
50 percent.

• Increase of suicide attempts at FEMA trailer parks—
79 percent.

• Largest private development project proposed—Jimmy
Buffett's Margarita-Ville Casino & Resort.

chapter 9

[198]

BEING WITH COLLIE is always both real and a bit blurry. Right now, my floor fan's blasting the features of her little face, lifting the sleeves and shoulders of her nightgown.

It's before dawn, at some wonderful hour.

We're stretched across the bed, playing Scrabble, or, nothing close to Scrabble, but we have the game out. That is, we did until someone shoved the board over the side. Perhaps we're too tired to play. I am.

Collie's there eating a carrot.

[199]

"What is this music?" Saunders asks as I load a disk into the player.

"Oh," I say, embarrassed, "it's just some stuff I Limewired."

"You do that?"

"Calm down," I say. "Not so much. Not all the time. Seven or eight thousand MP3s. Not like some people."

"Well, grab all you can. Do it while you're still young" he says.

"Yes, that's my feeling. I'm not still so young, however."

"You're what? Around forty?"

"That's correct. I am around forty. Not right around," I say.

[200]

Even they don't know that the skin on the palms of their hands, and along their forearms, and on their stomachs, their chests, throats, cheeks, at their temples, at the nape of their necks, and along their spines, at the small of their backs, behind their knees, along their thighs, and their calves, smells different at different times on each of them, but on either of them, it smells the same.

[201]

"So, you're thinking about going over the wall."

"Indeed," says Petal.

"Hoochie Coochie man," she says to an orderly wandering by.

"This is jive," I say. "You signed yourself in, voluntarily. I was standing right next to you. Therefore, you're permitted to leave whenever you like."

"No," she says, shaking her head.

"What could you mean, *no?*"

She says, "Here's how it goes. They wait 'til they've got you inside and got you medicated. Then, if ever you mention leaving, they tell you any discussion of that is premature, and then they rush out of the room. Same thing happens the next three or four times you bring it up. You say the word 'leaving,' they say 'premature,' and rush out of the room."

"Despite everything," I say, "it would be fun to be you."

She says, "The *fifth* time you ask, that's when they bash you with the insurance threat. If you leave against medical advice, the doctors won't sign off on you, the insurance provider won't pay, you're fucked."

"This is not my understanding of 'voluntary.'"

"Just forget voluntary," Petal says. "That's a ploy. It's meant to mislead you. It's like a lubricant they smear on you in Admissions."

[202]

"Cover yourself," I tell Lucien over the phone. "Wear the highest, thickest rubber boots that you can find. Wear a hat with earflaps. Serious gloves. Duct tape all your clothes to your skin. Leave no openings. Next, drench every part of you, as well as every piece of your clothing in Deet. Until you're saturated and dripping. Using however much Deet it takes. Then sit down somewhere, and let it soak into you, and do that for at least an *hour* before you go anywhere near the swamps."

[203]

Whatever else, I see flowers among the weeds—yarrow, and lavender, coral bells, black-eyed Susan, columbine, and purple heart, verbena. Deeply colored. Smelling so dear. Having such a lolly-dolly, mother-fucking good time.

[204]

The twins' mother, fresh from a shower and seated at her vanity mirror, swivels around slightly when I am let in. There are her good-looking legs, bare, crossed, showing at the opening of her long and white kimono, which is printed with iris blossoms.

She has a coffee service on the sideboard. French roast. I pour a cup, shake in sweetener, busy myself with test sips while I hang back. Trying to form a remark that won't make matters worse.

Her back's to me now, so I talk to her face in the oval mirror.

When I'm finished, she asks me, "Do *you* even believe what you're saying?" and watches my reflection, and listens to my answer or doesn't.

[205]

- No more questioning and shining the big flashlight on my husband at 4 A.M.
- I'm never again hiding from him underneath the car.
- No more will he persuade me to dance for drinks.

- I'm all done wearing his various shoes.

- No more sleepwalking episodes where I take a bubble bath in his parents' private tub.

- I'm finally through cigarette-burning my name onto his underwear.

[206]

The twins' father comes down the stairs and walks blandly past me. I follow him into his office. It's a room with cherry wood, and furnished in black and white.

He lets me stand at the center of the room while he rifles through some papers left on his desk. "Who does this?" he asks. Now he sits, tugs his buttoned vest straight, scoots forward in his chair. "What's on your mind?" he asks.

When I don't answer instantly he says, "I dislike guessing games"

I say, "It's starting to look as though you set something up with the Petal hospital. I mean, the psychiatric Petal. Clinic! The Saint Antoine's fucking Petal facility."

"Do you need to take a second?"

"No!"

Through his window I can see the white day and the sunlight frying the leaves of the several jacaranda trees there on the veranda.

"Eve," he says, and I feel the same surprise as if someone slapped me. "I'm sensitive about aggressive remarks. I warn you. I don't allow them."

"Aggressive. You don't allow them."

"Yes, I thought you—"

"I'm getting her a lawyer."

"Not with my money," he says, suddenly in such a rush. "I'll not finance that. Nor will my sons. She *made* her bed, and so did you, I might add."

"*I* earn money."

He shrugs his shoulders. "Oh? Well, good, then. You'll have no problem."

"Bubba fuck," I say instead of goodbye.

[207]

"You can at least take me to see Brad Pitt," says Kip, the producer. "He's in the Holy Cross neighborhood, I think someone said. And the Musicians' Village, that's another must, if Harry Connick and Brad Marsalis are going to be there. What about your director friend Michael Almereyda? He did a film of this, didn't he? Give him a call. I'm assuming you know where to find Ms. Jolie. Even little things about her schedule would be good to learn. I'm sure they're through finding bodies? I heard you can still see dogs' skeletons that were tangled up in the power lines. I mean, the *smell* in these areas must be ungodly."

My thoughts are on my fingers. I'm checking how far each of them will bend back.

[208]

Smash & Grab are here to join us for lunch.

"You gotta tell me which one's your husband," says Kip.

"Umm, kind of have to ask *them*," I say.

As they arrive at the table, Kip says, "You two look fine to me. I thought one of you was sick or something."

"Sick," says Adam, raising a finger.

"I must be Something," says Saunders.

Kip doesn't take any time out for them. And he's stopped bothering with the smile, I notice.

"So, let me ask you. When they're down in the trenches," he says, "do Pitt and Jolie use a special trailer or something? It'd be great if I got a shot of them going in and out of a port-a-john. I'm going to want plenty of pictures. Not to sell, but to show to people."

His face is flushed and stung-looking now. I'm sorry for him, but not much.

"Adam," says the nearer twin, half rising from his seat and reaching to shake hands.

So we have that one little thing straight for today.

When he and Kip finish shaking, Saunders tosses Adam a dinner napkin to wipe his hand.

"And then I've got alcohol in the car," Saunders says.

I nod to that. "Bottles and bottles."

[209]

We are in the front room of the FEMA trailer Lucien inhabits. I see a few sorrowful furnishings in a non-descript room.

Lucien's in a cornice, speaking into a land phone, ordering medication from a pharmacy, it sounds like. He spells the drug's name out slowly, pauses, spells it out slowly again.

He finishes, stands with his hands bunched in his pockets.

It's not great for him, my being here, I can tell. He looks pinched, and stepped on, and as if he thinks maybe the police are on the way.

The walls in here are making everything more crowded.

On this hot and scratchy day that's almost at an end.

[210]

We're strolling in the Vieux Carré, Lucien and I. There are headlights and streetlamps and neon signs coming on, and marquees with female figures depicted in red and purple and yellow and orange. There are greetings and salutations and horn music winding all around.

Lucien plucks something from his thigh pocket and shows me—a note with a hand-printed list. He says, "I found this, this morning, and it's somebody's grocery list, all right?"

"I would think so."

"But I gotta wonder, why did this particular piece of paper choose to descend upon *me*? Until I felt like, the only obvious conclusion is, buy every item on the list."

[211]

There's a baseball game on television now. Saunders says, "'O'er the ramparts we watch.' Is this not a source of frustration for people? Why not something clear and comprehensible? Like, oh country, full of diesel trucks and all different birds. There's a lot of crap and faults but it's where I live anyway."

[212]

"You better run!" I shout at the parents' boxer dog. "And just re-member, there's a scary, dog-eating bitch after you!"

Saunders says, "Hmm. You ought to be stingier with your adjectives when our mother's out there in the hall."

[213]

* Rake is the angle at which your holster holds your gun.

* Neutral Rake has your gun at a vertical and will work well on either side, but won't necessarily facilitate a faster draw.

* Small-of-the-Back Holsters can benefit from Butt Forward Rake, as it allows for a palm-out draw.

* Butt Forward Rake is also right for an easy, rapid draw from a Cross Draw Holster. However, in close situations, a Butt Forward Rake could make your gun dangerously accessible to your enemy.

- Muzzle Forward/Butt Rear Rake, known as the FBI Tilt, is the perfect choice for a Strong Side Holster.
- Muzzle Forward Rake is also excellent for keeping your gun hidden. The holster, at this angle, tucks the butt nicely into the band of flesh at your waist.

[214]

Up front, a fellow in patient's pajamas is slowly, one cautious step at a time, sneaking out of the room.

Bounding after him is a jumbo nurse, maybe male, maybe female.

On the television here in the back, political people, seated face-to-face, are shouting out loud at one another.

Petal's curled up beside me on the couch, dopey and giggly and speaking in singsong.

"All right, people," calls out the giant nurse. "Come on now. "It's nightie night. Tell everybody bye-bye."

[215]

I get a call and it's the producer sounding brassy and miniatured and inquiring about where to go tonight to hear music and have some fun.

This is tempting. A right answer would be start at Preservation Hall in the Quarter, move on to the Dragon's Den above the

Siam Cafe on Esplanade, then on to Snug Harbor and the Spotted Cat on Frenchmen Street, but leave before too late and end up at Sweet Lorraine's in the back of Marigny. There are assorted wrong answers.

[216]

"Lucien," I say, "here are the things to know if you're a good location scout:

Are there time requirements for getting in and out? The answer's no. Lord, no.

Is there a specified date when they have to finish and strike the sets? No.

Accessibility. What's that going to be like for their equipment? Plenty of accessibility.

Noise factors? Remarkably none.

Traffic and blocking off roads. Say, it's been taken care of, or *well* taken care of. How about construction? That's on the sound issue again. No construction anywhere close by.

Air traffic. You don't foresee a problem.

Sensitivity of the place. That's to what degree may they ruin everything. Pass this question along. It's all covered in the documents between the lawyers and insurance folk.

Food and services. Caterers, lunch tents, a First Aid person. Blow these questions off too. Say the agency governs that stuff.

Parking? Show them a diagram. Any diagram, at this point. They're never going to remember.

Shuttle times, for getting to and from the set. Always say it takes eighteen minutes. Or no, always say it usually takes you eighteen minutes."

[217]

We're in the main parlor, Buy Now & Pay Later, their parents, and I. It's a white room with archways and plaster frieze work. There are Italian Majolica vases exploding with red and white blooms. The doors are open to the veranda and the later afternoon air is arriving, warm and sad and lovely.

I would like to get out of here, nevertheless. It's just hard to leave when the parents are sitting there, wishing I would.

"I don't care for any horse in the third race," says Adam. Not *to* anyone really. So this is a worry.

He and his brother look a little like twin Kurt Cobains tonight. That's if Kurt Cobain had been dragged by a car for another fifteen years.

The father would hit me, if no one would ever know. And earlier today, the mother followed me until I turned on her and shouted, "I'm not going to steal!"

They have no real reason to hate me in particular. I didn't waste Saunders or give Adam Hep-C. Rather, the parents should hate the twins. The twins should hate the parents. The twins should also hate each other, come to think of it, along a couple of lines. Else wise, everyone should just try and take it easy.

I'm watching the sick son there in his white and beautiful dinner jacket, and the ruined son, who's been trying for a while now to wedge his flask into his handkerchief pocket.

[218]

At twilight, Saunders ambles out of the little cypress tree forest behind the parents' house, bare-chested and carrying an amber drink in a tall, thin glass.

"Ah, a Tom Collins," I say.

"A highball," he says, "you silly."

"I need you for something, Saunders. A lift home. Because your folks are your folks and they live here. So the only choice is for me to run."

He tilts his highball glass at my mouth and gives me a sloshing sip.

"Sweet Aunt Josephine," I say.

He says, "This is why driving, for me, is a problem."

"What if *I* were to drink all the rest?"

"You'd have my respect. You'd go into shock, maybe."

"My question's about you."

"I would have to go mix another."

I say, "I meant, if you were to drink no more."

"Let's just put you into a nice taxi cab," he says. "There are still cabs in this city, aren't there?"

"I know there are men who will *call* their cars cabs," I say. "Free of charge, usually, but provided you'll go wherever they want you to go."

He puts his arm on my shoulder and says, "We'll sit out on the driveway. Like we're in a dream."

[219]

We roll on the lawn. He pulls me under him, and drags off some of my clothes. There's plenty of darkness. There's a candy smell. The only light is in flashes of heat lightning. There's the faintest sound of far-off people laughing. What a place this is. God almighty. The amenities you can count on.

[220]

I've been walking around in the dewy yard since Saunders wandered off toward the house to fetch his bourbon.

He's coming back along the path now, having forgotten the bourbon, it would seem. He did, however, bring his white dinner jacket to throw over me.

We move into the cover of a mangrove tree that's strung with vines. I lean and kiss his throat.

He says, "I'm not sure I wanna be out here. Don't you think we'd do better inside?"

"Oh, that's too tricky," I say. "Adam might be awake."

He shudders, and stands off, nodding his head. "Madam, I'm Adam," he says with no life in his voice.

[221]

"You just drive blind," I say to him after a while. "Because you find that you *can,* for a bit. That the road's usually straight, and there are no monsters in it usually, or ditches to fall down."

"Until the time there is and you do," says my husband, and I say, "Until the time you do."

[222]

The City That Care Forgot

- The oceans are getting higher and warmer, as New Orleans continues to sink.

- The wetlands are eroding at a rate of 2 football fields an hour.

- 2,100 square miles of land and barrier islands have melted into the sea.

• According to the Army Corps of Engineers, the city will
be safe from storms by 2011, but will not be safe from
storms as severe as Katrina.

[223]

I'm leaving quietly now and don't suppose I'm ever coming back,
creeping away in my car, past the pond where the sister drowned,
where the black swans circle, where the statue wades.

Hit the brakes. That miserable goddamn pond. What belongs at
the bottom of it is Petal's gun.

I snatch it from the glove compartment, hop out the car. Walk
fifteen feet. Wind my arm and swing high.

The gun wangs toward the water, and, smashing into the statue's
face, goes off. One of the swans explodes.

[224]

I'm lying on the ground in the dark among the mosses and flowering
plants.

Someone's coming now, running on the path. I am caught.

On that side of the fence, the NOPD arrives. They pop from their
patrol car, weapons drawn.

It's Adam standing over me, I'm just about sure. Here to see how
I've puked more thoroughly on his evening.

I stay on the ground but yell at the police: "Never mind! You can go away! I am not the neighbor kids!"

In answer, they're firing their guns at me.

A shot lifts Adam into the air, punches him backward onto the grass.

I lift up a little, to see.

None of this is right, though. None of it. This is *animation*, a cartoon of Adam on his back. They don't even have the face the way it should be. It's pushed up above a blood-geyser-ing *mess* at the top of his chest. I don't accept any of it. It's wrong. Patently wrong, they can do it over.

I'm *walking* in blood that's coming from *me* now. Way to goddamn fucking go. They managed to get it to where I'm providing the blood.

This night does look awfully familiar, though. Icicle lights? Those're pretty good. And, I don't know whose they are, but a hundred falsetto voices saying, "Eleven P.M.! Eleven P.M.!"

[225]

If I were really going anywhere, I'd need to be there around ten. I'd be forty-five minutes late by now! *If* I were really going anywhere, and doing what I'm supposed to. All that I promised, and rather publicly were they made, some of those promises. Instead, I'm riding away.

There are med techs here in the back with me, but they don't seem prepared to act. I don't know how to counsel them. The driver or somebody else up front is calling in, and saying, "One DOA, one on the way. We've got one DOA. Another on the way."

I tell ya!

Ah, but at least tonight, we get to ride in the real ambulance. With a siren. Carrying us somewhere. I believe the Trauma Center is open. They better double check. See if the Trauma Center hasn't evaporated. Because I am fairly sure. But still. These days. It's so very hard to know.